C. L. DONLEY

The King's Vizier

Contents

1

Chapter 1

King Belkacem al Malwali patiently waited at the top of the stairs of Ghassan's embassy.

His half-brother and vizier stood on one side of him, his interpreter was on the other. Intermittent sounds of camera shutters could be heard as Bel stood quietly in front of a smattering of press. Stiffly engaged in small talk, the King was well aware of the camera crew that also accompanied them in the drab conference room dotted with dark marble pillars and lined with national flags.

The king of Ghassan's neighboring country and ally, Manaf, was expected to arrive to discuss a sensitive matter. Bel had assumed it was merely a dignified excuse to hang, but the pomp and circumstance of meeting at the borders of their countries suggested this wasn't something that could be handled over the phone.

The last time Bel had spoken to King Khoury had been at a party for a certain Saudi prince, held at a resort in Qatar. King Khoury was still unmarried, so it was common for royalty from other smaller monarchies to entertain him in an effort to seduce him into an alliance. It'd been the year after Manafi soldiers shot down his father's concubine and her family at the border of their countries, and the young King Khoury had expressed stoic remorse. Bel had smiled and reassured him again that retaliation was the furthest from his mind.

When Bel saw the handsome king approach the embassy steps while he was still a ways off, his smile was back.

The Africans that'd settled in Manaf so long ago must've been a single tribe with strong genes, because they all looked the same, no matter how many Arabs they mixed with. Manaf's Queen Mother had been from the Ivory Coast, so the king was destined to be tall and sculpted.

Black James Bond was Khoury's name in Bel's head. The Queen had once called him a "human jungle gym" and he hadn't taken it well.

Camera shutters snapped in a flurry once King Khoury rushed up the steps to meet his good friend and greet him with a warm hug. The two men utilized their translators as a courtesy. And also, to make the press work harder. Western press never bothered to translate what they were actually saying.

"The Queen won't be joining us this evening?" Emir asked with a smile, waiting for his interpreter to finish.

"She sends her regards," Bel smiled. "I was under the impression this meeting required discretion."

"It does, but I was looking forward to enjoying her delightful manner and beauty."

"She is indeed delightful," Bel laughed in Farsi. "But whatever sensitive information you have to share wouldn't stand a chance in her presence."

King Emir Khoury had become king of Manaf at the young age of eight. The people loved him, and Bel's own father had taken to the boy king during his tenure (for tactical purposes, of course). Now King Khoury was all grown up— still young at 28 but had been a king a full 16 years longer than Bel had been when he took the throne four years ago. So in a way, Bel looked up to him.

The men discussed diplomatic matters once they retreated inside to a large narrow conference room, each of their Generals conducting business while the press looked on, waiting to shoot something they could print.

"I've been meaning to ask you about your time in America," the young king asked Bel when they were alone.

"America?" Bel grinned.

"How were you able to move freely in America for so long without anyone suspecting your father was the King of Ghassan?"

"America is obscenely large and ignorant of most things happening outside of its borders, especially anything beyond mother Europe," replied Bel.

"What about your enemies at home?"

"If I'd known I had them, that my father was keeping sensitive matters from his own advisors, I would have acted differently. But the throne never went unoccupied," Bel mused, making himself a cup of tea.

"Obviously, once I became King, I had to leave America for good." Bel's gray eyes gleamed. "But surely you didn't ask me here so formally to reminisce about my old life."

King Khoury poured himself a glass of Brandy as he continued in English.

"My vizier has come across some most unusual information," he said. "He tells me that an heir to the Ashwari throne lives in America."

Bel raised an eyebrow. Now that was intriguing news indeed.

Ashwari was a small country off the East African coast, not even an hour's boat ride away from King Khoury in Manaf and the home of Emir's mother. Bel's father was betrothed to an Ashwari princess when he was a teen. That didn't work out. Especially after he met Bel's mother.

It was currently embroiled in religious warfare, the kind of conflict the East African Coast was unacquainted with. Ashwari, it seemed, was overrun with bad luck. Bad luck that stemmed from an unholy alliance between the surrounding nations that had sucked it dry— with the help of their notoriously corrupt king—before either of them was born.

"America, you say? How distant an heir?" Bel asked, pouring himself more tea.

"Otieno's daughter."

Bel stopped short of a sip.

"Impossible."

"One of my mother's old attendants swore under oath that they helped smuggle her out of the country during the uprising. Right before my father was killed," King Khoury replied.

"How could they smuggle the princess out of the country without King Otieno knowing?"

"Otieno knew of it," King Khoury said adjusting his posture. "The Queen traveled with her daughter and governess to visit America and left the Princess with relatives. Apparently, the Queen went to seek asylum, and simply did not come back with the Princess when she was denied," Khoury said.

"Otieno let the Queen travel alone?"

"The Queen was attempting to escape her husband, so she simply defied him and left. He apparently intended to have her punished once she returned. But the rebellion erupted."

4

"So, smuggling the Princess to America had nothing to do with Ashwari's government being overthrown."

"Precisely."

Bel gave his head a solitary shake as he put his teacup down. Clever bastard.

"It makes me wonder whether Otieno kept that little piece of intel to the grave."

"The Queen certainly would have. The attendant of my mother says another baby girl was killed in her stead. A gruesome detail. This convinced me it was valid."

"I'm beginning to remember," King Belkacem leaned forward in his chair. "One of your father's first orders of business was to ally with Ashwari. The two of you were betrothed, his offspring, and you. I recall my father being worried your two countries would attack us."

"Perhaps that was the plan, before my father's untimely assassination," King Khoury replied without emotion. "I even recall her visit to the palace. At least, I assume it was her. I was very young myself. Well before my king days."

Manaf had been antsy these last ten years or so that King Khoury had dragged his feet finding a suitable queen. Knowing him, Bel had to assume that this could only be, in the words of his good friend back in the States, *some Coming to America shit.*

"You want to find her and marry her," deduced Bel.

Emir relinquished a shy smile, lowering his eyes. "How did you know?"

"It seems logical," Belkacem lightly shrugged.

King Khoury's black eyes looked grim as he twirled the liquor-filled tumbler in his hands, considering the task ahead.

"Ashwari is in ruins. Nothing like the lush coastal paradise I remember. It was the Queen Mother's dying wish to see it restored."

"Is there anyone alive that even remembers it under Otieno?"

"Of course. The people are afraid to openly denounce the usurper. If he can be publicly unseated by Otieno's rightful heir, the people will have hope."

"You'll have to find her quickly and marry her even quicker. Not to mention bring her safely home without causing suspicion. Olayinka hunted and killed every last heir down to the once-removed cousin."

"Which is why I need your help."

"You'll have my support in whatever way you need," Bel raised his brow warily, "but be warned. If the Princess has spent her life in America, she may not want to come back with you. Even if it means being a Princess," he continued between sips. "America is a prosperous country. Liberal. The women enjoy many more freedoms there."

"I've been made aware of the challenges by my vizier."

Bel gave the black, aromatic liquid a clamorous stir in his hand with a sterling silver teaspoon, clinking against the china. "I trust this will be... an authentic marriage?" Bel teased.

If King Khoury knew Bel's mischievous intent, he didn't let on. Emir was always a bit on the nose.

"It must be," he answered. "I've been under pressure to produce heirs my entire reign. I no longer wish to burden the country of Manaf with the future of the Khoury line."

Bel squinted in amusement. "Have you never fallen in love, your Majesty?"

"I have tried," King Khoury confessed. "By the time I was a man, I'd already been a king for many years. Women have only ever been little more than a mild amusement. Nothing to relinquish half of my kingdom for."

"But a Princess," Bel deduced, "*the* Princess. Of a country in need of hope."

"In truth, I desire her already," Emir declared, "for what she represents."

Bel smiled. "You even have the turn-ons of a king."

"Otieno was obsessed with women. The former queen was a great beauty. I'm confident that producing heirs won't be much of a chore," King Khoury reasoned mechanically. Though inwardly he'd been creating mental composites of her since he was given the news.

"She must be of age by now," the King said.

"Twenty-five, by my calculations."

"Older than most Manafi brides," Bel volunteered.

"That is true," Khoury conceded. "But in my limited experiences, modern women take much longer to mature. In America even more so, I imagine."

"The thought of you going to America amuses me greatly, Emir," King Belkacem casually addressed him. "You will hate it, but it will do you good. You are far too handsome to be so severe."

"I was a severe child. I am now a severe man."

"Becoming king has changed me a great deal," Belkacem mused in his native Farsi. "I have imagined myself as a boy in your shoes many nights. Manaf is thriving because you have given yourself to it. You deserve to see the world."

King Khoury's eye twinkled affectionately.

"I hear every man is king in America," he offered as he sat forward in the study's chair, elbows on his haunches.

"The country is truly great, there is no doubt," Bel confessed. "Many have tried to plunder it, to crumble it from within but it perseveres." Bel pointed with his dainty spoon, the sleeves of

7

his silk shirt slightly rolled. "Your Princess has Otieno's blood, but make no mistake. She is undoubtedly American through and through."

Khoury nodded with a contemplative look, his natural smolder on display. "Mazigh was educated there. He has warned me that she may be... insolent. Combative."

"American women are a mixed bag," Bel tilted his head. "But the recipe for a noble character is the same everywhere."

"He tells me not every man is obligated to fight, so the men are as soft as women," King Khoury divulged. "Some have not seen war for generations. The individual is praised above all else in America. At the expense of family duty and responsibility."

Bel put down his glass, measuring his response. "In America, a man can truly test what he is made of, no matter his station. In every man's eyes, I was no one. Even with my father's connections, I was the equivalent of a merchant. I blended into every crowd. The possibilities are truly seductive to many whose destinies have been predetermined by birth at home. Many who were born there do not, of course, feel this same need."

"Would you have ever come home, Belkacem?" asked Khoury, genuinely curious. "Had your father lived and your General took the throne as planned?"

Bel thought for a moment with a slight shake of his head. "I don't know. But I was glad for the need to come home. I will openly admit I indulged in everything America had to offer until I was numb. I had no responsibilities. Most Americans do not have the luxury of making such mistakes."

Emir rested one leg across the other, sitting back. "I'm in no danger of America's seduction. I simply need to extract the Queen and bring her to her ancestral home."

"She'll need to be educated. About where and who she comes

from."

"Perhaps Queen Kimberly can assist in acquainting her with royal life?"

"She would be honored," Bel smiled, pouring himself a third cup of still-steaming tea. "You say your vizier was educated there. Would it not be simpler to entrust him to retrieve her? He's fought alongside mine on several occasions. Surely he can be entrusted with this."

"He can. But I would much rather handle this matter personally."

Bel nodded his head this way and that, brainstorming. "You could travel to America under the guise of diplomacy. A vacation. Anything, really. Olayinka and his men would suspect nothing, of course. But you could still draw too much attention from the press, who are forever starving for information to share. The enemy of covert operations. Especially in the company of your royal guard."

"Then I will go alone."

Bel gave one smooth shake of his head. "The King of Manaf traveling without protection to America will certainly arouse suspicion." His brow furrowed as he strategized. "Besides, you might overwhelm the girl. She is liable to have you arrested."

"I was thinking of a more... covert approach."

"More covert than traveling alone unguarded?"

King Khoury set his tumbler down. "The King's vizier is skilled in extraction missions."

"Extraction? As in... kidnapping?" Bel confirmed, sounding distressed.

"We don't have time for re-education," King Khoury flatly stated.

"Surely you can convince the girl to come along with you

willingly. Not to mention, the intel of her story must be verified before you go kidnapping an American," Bel replied, amused.

King Khoury breathed in and out impatiently. What was the danger, exactly? America was impossibly large, and people disappeared all the time. His vizier knew the terrain. He was positive they could track down the girl and slip her a sedative that wouldn't wear off until they were in the air again.

But he had to defer to the King of Ghassan, who seemed to know better.

"Manaf does not yet have an American embassy," Bel remembered. "Perhaps you could kill two birds with one stone? The short notice would only strike them as peculiar, at best. Likely too late to meet with anyone higher than the Speaker of the House, but that would be what you want. The president would draw too many eyes. Were the timing better, the Queen and I would accompany you. But as it stands, we can only wish you a safe journey there and back. I trust you'll be leaving soon?"

"As soon as possible," the King urgently replied.

"Send your guard ahead of you, but you and your vizier can take my plane. Split the difference."

Belkacem cocked his head in realization, his smokey gray eyes inquisitive. "Did the old woman say where they left the girl?"

King Khoury searched his memory.

"A place called... Tampa."

Chapter 2

"Mrs. Holderman hold still!" Gabby clenched.

"Get offa me, you black bitch!" Mrs. Holderman screamed.

Woooosah, Gabby thought in her head as she and another nurse helped restrain a squirming Mrs. Holderman. They weren't wrong when they said service hours were when the real education starts.

Mrs. Holderman was Gabby's twenty-sixth patient at Sunnyside Nursing Home. She wasn't the most advanced stage dementia patient, but she was the most unpredictable. When she wasn't being the kindest, sweetest soul on the planet, she was raging about the smallest thing and spitting directly in Gabby's face.

She loved her job, but if it wasn't for the fact that Mrs. Holderman wouldn't let a single other nurse take care of her, Gabby would gladly skip this part of the day. At least it wasn't hard 'r' n-words this afternoon.

"All done Mrs. Holderman," Gabby announced when her body was cleaned and her shot administered.

"Well, that's a relief. No thanks to *you*," was Mrs. Holderman's semi-coherent statement.

"I better not find any more empty honey packets between those sheets. Dinner's at the same time every night, you know that."

"Leave me alone, corn pone!" snapped Mrs. Holderman.

Gabby and Sara, the other CNA, left Mrs. Holderman's door cracked as they quietly left.

"Another hellish day," Sara sighed.

"Honestly, I've had worse days."

"You know, Vicki told me we're not even supposed to be administering medication as CNA's?"

"Pretty sure we're not supposed to be scrubbing the floors or making the pancakes, but here we are," Gabby shrugged.

"I can't *wait* until I'm done here. I already know long-term care just isn't for me," Sara rolled her calico gray eyes. Sara was a smooth medium brown, a shade class lighter than Gabby's with fuller lips and a prominent nose. She didn't know much beyond her family's descriptions of their old life in Ashwari, but Gabby knew enough to know that had Sara been born there, she would've been a queen.

"Really? Hospital nursing's way worse to me," Gabby insisted.

"How can you say that?"

"It's a nightmare. All those people coming in and out," she said, their soundless blue and green scrubs and sneakers squeaking down the fluorescent lighted hallway.

"Yeah, but at most you're only juggling six patients a day. Not *twenty*-six," Sara argued.

"It's non-stop chaos and you're expected to keep up with it all."

"Gabby, I swear, some of the shit you say. You just described your current position," Sarah chuckled, grabbing a chart at the station.

"Yeah, but you get to know the patients here, you get to be part of their routine," rallied Gabby.

"Which is the very reason why I can't with this job. How am I supposed to learn how to do this if I'm doing the same damn thing every day?" Sara complained in a hushed tone. "I did the math, you know. I'm paying $153 a day to be here, and I feel like I haven't learned anything but the basics."

"There's something to be said for mastering the basics," Gabby defended. Gabby grabbed a clipboard and a cart, heading up the stairs.

"There's *also* something to be said for coming across every possible scenario so that you can be the best nurse you can possibly be."

"I hear that. I guess I just feel this is like, the most impactful."

"And I think it's the opposite," Sara made her point emphatically as she divvied out meds in plastic cups on the cart.

"Well then, I guess we each got our shit figured out."

"We do," Sara agreed with a sassy tone. "Plus, I'm tryna get this money."

"Listen, I'm not gonna complain," Gabby said, half distracted. She checked off the patients' names carefully, double-checking doses. "$15.88 to cook and clean is more than my mama makes to do the same damn thing."

"Girl, if you're still at this raggedy-ass place when we graduate, I'm gonna break your legs," Sara threatened.

Gabby felt a tinge of guilt leaving all the patients behind that she'd cultivated relationships with for the past six months. Who would take care of Mrs. Holderman while she was gone? She wouldn't let the other nurses come near her.

"Here's hoping Mrs. Holderman goes on to glory before I graduate," Gabby sighed, knocking on the first door.

"My money's on the other place," Sarah muttered.

Gabby gave Sarah a smack on the arm as they politely entered the first patient's room on the second floor.

* * *

When their shift ended, Sara and Gabby parted ways across the parking lot, keys to the old gray Honda in Gabby's hand. She'd finally convinced her parents to let her drive to school, work, and back. Her parents had been scared stiff to let her drive ever since she got her license.

In Florida, you were able to obtain a license as an undocumented immigrant, but that did not put her parents at ease who, even though *they* were legal, insisted on living life like a Tom Clancy movie.

At 25, she'd only been driving for three years, and before Uber that was embarrassing. You needed a car to get everywhere in Tampa. Her brother and sister didn't mind driving her around, but having to rely on her younger sister— who was more popular and outgoing than she ever was— sometimes strained their relationship.

"Mom, I'm home!" Gabby announced from the front door. She couldn't see her mom but she was most certainly somewhere in the house, wondering who'd just come from the front door if Gabby hadn't just yelled it out. Her brother Faraj was on the couch watching the news of all things:

And in Washington today, White House officials met with King Khoury of Manaf to discuss diplomatic relations and the possible addition of a U.S. embassy to its nation. Manaf, border country to both Ghassan and Saudi Arabia, is one of only seven nations in the U.N. that does not yet have an American embassy within its borders...

"Since when do you care about current affairs?" Gabby teased.

"Shh..." was Faraj's curt, distracted response. Faraj was older than her by three years and looked a bit like Peele from Key & Peele, but slim and slightly darker. At 28, he still wasn't married yet, much to their family's dismay. He must be here for dinner, Gabby deduced.

"Go help your sister in the kitchen," her mother's disembodied voice floated from the laundry room at the back of the shotgun-style house. "Your father will be home soon."

"I'm hopping in the shower, I'll be right there," Gabby said to her sister on the way to her room.

"Convenient!" Mackenzie shouted from the kitchen, cutting up the last of the vegetables prepared to go into a boiling stew pot on the stove.

Gabby's sister Mackenzie would be graduating high school this year. Going to the University of Central Florida. Gabby tried to let her happiness for her sister drown out her resentment and sorrow, and for the most part, succeeded.

Long before it was time for her to go, she'd been sending off for informational pamphlets from the universities of her choice. It was her own little obsession since she was thirteen. For her, college had been her jumping-off point, that catalyst that would take her out of her strict, close-knit community and get her noticed.

When she began applying, her parents finally caved and told her the real reason for their overprotective behaviors: that she was undocumented. Her life's plans came crashing down in an instant.

There would be no college, no following her best friend

Carmen to Florida State, no coming home on weekends and holidays. No finding a college boyfriend. No further education whatsoever.

That is until Gabby bothered to do her research.

She offered to work for several years, save up enough money for community college, and go into a high-demand field where there was an opportunity for an employer-assisted green card.

Thankfully, Florida was covered with such programs for nurses. Only then could she convince her parents that she was safe.

"Gabby!"

Before she could get on her pink shower cap with the purple flowers, her sister Mackenzie had come barreling through the door. Good Lord, she couldn't wait until *one* of them finally left home for good.

"Mom wants to know if you invited Tek and Savaday to dinner," was Mackenzie's supremely *un*-urgent question. Savaday and Tek were two boys from their small Ashwari community that had formed in Tampa. The older generation was constantly trying to hook up all their offspring up with each other. And in a very boring turn of events, they'd mostly succeeded.

"What? Why would I do that?" Gabby echoed across the shower curtain.

"Mom says they've just pulled up."

Weird.

"Savaday's here to see you, not me. He gave up on me, remember?" Gabby sneered. "Maybe he's here for you. Now that you're 18 and all."

"He better not be," Mackenzie sucked her teeth. "Maybe he changed his mind. Why would he come here unannounced? Do you think he wants to propose?"

"Ew, get *outta* here with all that! And close the door, you're letting in all the cold air!" Gabby huffed with her soapy eyes tightly shut.

Gabby was losing patience with her living arrangement, which troubled her because she honestly didn't know what else she would do if she wasn't living at home. Part of her didn't even feel comfortable calling it "home" anymore. Ever since the truth about her illegal status had come out, her parents seemed more and more like strangers.

Even after they came to an agreement about community college, Gabby's questions to her parents continued until it came to a head. She could no longer explain away the fact that she was illegal while her parents and siblings were not. How was it that she could not receive federal funding, that she would have to pay the out-of-state amount of tuition for a community college, and only get a non-compliant driver's license?

The simple fact was that she must have been born in their native Ashwari, not here in America. And that the two people that raised her could not be her parents.

After the only shouting match of her life, her mother broke down and told her that they'd kidnapped her. But even that seemed like a lie.

Gabby stepped out of the shower, wiped off the mirror, and looked at herself with a sigh. She was now in her mid-20's, and yet she still felt nothing like an adult. Unbelievably stifled. She distantly heard more than just her brother's booming voice in the living room, but it hardly registered. She was too busy feeling overwhelmed.

The lifelong superstition and paranoia engrained in her made it hard for Gabby to even take the first steps toward legitimate citizenship without the threat of deportation.

While she was glad her parents allowed her to grow up without the burden of knowing her illegal status, she resented that they'd saddled her adulthood with it. Almost as if they didn't have a plan. As if they'd been ready at any moment—

"*Asha!*"

Gabby jumped at the sound of her mother calling her by her Ethiopian name, which usually meant mortal danger. Or that she'd neglected her chores and Father was home.

But she resented the implication. She'd been at school all day and not yet home ten minutes. But she knew that she had exactly 3.5 seconds to show herself if she wanted to escape discipline.

"*Yes, Ema!*" she answered in Amharic, to show respect in lieu of her appearance.

She was still soaking wet, wearing her pink and purple shower cap, and couldn't find something to cover up with fast enough. She settled on wrapping a towel around her tall, skinny frame and ventured barefoot out of the bathroom and into the hallway.

As steam barreled out of the door and into the hall, Gabby could just make out the living room that suddenly seemed to be filled with an audience. Whatever her mother had beckoned her about, it wasn't chores.

She hesitated, still trying to make out what she was seeing. Everything was deathly quiet and the air was that of reverence. Authority. She didn't know who was here, but it sure as shit wasn't Savaday. Or Tek.

Was it the police? Were they coming to take her away?

She stiffened. Oh no. Nononono.

If this were truly her last hour in this country, she would never forgive herself for forcing her parents to allow her more freedom.

She felt her mother grab her forcefully by the arms and pull her into the adjacent bedroom, which was her sister's room. She slammed the door behind her and put her hand over Gabby's mouth.

"Do...not... scream," her mother said in a calm voice.

Gabby simply made a slow gesture with one hand as she furrowed her brow. Her mother removed her hand.

"What would I be screaming about, exactly?" Gabby asked.

"About who is here. About what I have to tell you."

Gabby wrinkled her brow. "What do you have to tell me?"

3

Chapter 3

Gabby's mother breathed as if vomitous, bracing herself. "I am not your biological mother. And your father, he is not your father."

"I know that," Gabby replied unphased.

"Okay," her mother nodded, not bothering to be surprised. She seemed as eager to air out the truth as Gabby was to hear it, which relieved her.

"I am... I was... your mother's best friend," she confessed, a solitary tear rolling down her cheek. "Your mother was like my sister. When you were a baby, she came here to visit us. And then she told us..."

Gabby's "mother" couldn't go on. She covered her mouth, tears streaming from her high dark cheeks. Gabby's own eyes began to water. Whatever the truth was, it was bad. Worse than she could imagine.

"*Ema* don't," Gabby insisted, jarred by her mother's emotion. "Just tell me who is here."

She shook her head in protest. "You won't understand. Until you know what happened."

Gabby's mood turned sober and dread blanketed her. Her heart thumped the more she entertained a new worst-case scenario.

"Are they here to take me away?" Gabby's voice quaked.

At that, her mother actually nodded, which struck fear in Gabby. But oddly, her mother's face was serene and smiling. Gabby's breath quickened.

"Mom, what's going on? Where are they taking me?"

"It's good, *mare*. Listen to me. You cannot stay here—"

"Mom, please—"

"Your father and I, we have not told *anyone* about you. Not a soul. Our connection to Ashwari is dead. And yet, these men are here, do you understand what that means?"

"...No, I don't."

"It means that if they can find out, then *he* can find out," her mother filled in cryptically. "The longer you stay here the more you're in danger."

"Who's 'he'? Why are you letting them take me?" Gabby began to panic.

The woman she knew as her mother was talking crazy. She wanted to hand her over to strange men. Would her father not fight for her?

Suddenly, she heard the unmistakable sound of him coming home.

"*Baba!*"

Gabby's mom put her hand back over her mouth. Gabby began trying to squirm out of her grasp.

"Gabby listen to me!" she whisper-yelled over her struggling. "Your name is Princess Asha Gabrielle Otieno. Your father was King Otieno of Ashwari."

When Gabby finally fell still, her mother removed her hand.

Gabby stared at her and stayed quiet.

"My name is Gabrielle Ayenew," she finally replied, confused.

The woman shook her head mournfully. "No. Your mother was Queen Aida Otieno of Ashwari. She came here to visit us, but when she got here she told me of her plan. She wanted to remain here, to seek asylum from your father, the King. When she could not get it, she left you with us and returned home. Where she died."

Her mother? Was a queen?

Her actual mother had been here? In America?

And she left her?

"Why did she leave?" Gabby asked with a lump in her throat.

"Because the King expected her back."

"Why? She would've been safe here. How would the King have even known to come here?"

"She told him plainly where she was going. That she was visiting family here, so the King would not try to chase her. And coming back without you bought her time. She was going to tell the King that we wished to keep you for a while. I assume that is what she did."

"*Stupid!*" Gabby replied in Amharic. A tear of anguish fell. "No government would've let us go back there. Ashwari is in ruins even now. You said it yourself!"

"Harboring the Queen of another country would've certainly caused a war with your father in charge," her fake mom explained. "Ashwari's allies killed him! And now they back his traitorous army General, who betrayed him and staged a coup! And killed every living Otieno in the land!"

"Except us?" Gabby gulped.

"Except *you*," her mother whispers, smoothing Gabby's hair with her hands. "Do you know what this means, *mare*? You are a queen!"

A queen? Gabby's brow knit even more and her eyes darted in confusion.

"I still don't understand. Why are the police here?"

"Those men are not the police," replied her mother.

"Then who are they?"

"Get dressed. I will let them explain."

When Gabby finally emerged from her room in a black over-sized sweatsuit from her sister's closet, the hood hiding her hair, her mother frowned. Meanwhile, her father had a beaming smile of pride on his face.

Her siblings had also gathered in the living room and looked somberly in her direction as if they'd announced she was dying.

Finally, she laid eyes on the two black men sitting at the dining room table, elegantly out of place and impeccably dressed in long coats far too warm for a Florida spring. Both men eyed her intently before looking at each other in unspoken decision.

Gabby sat on the arm of the floral living room couch with arms crossed, waiting to hear the day's bizarre events unfold. The man in the camel-colored coat spoke first.

"You are in the presence of King Emir Khoury, son of Kamau Khoury, King of Manaf. I am the king's vizier. My name is Mazigh Chike. You can call me Max."

Manaf... she'd heard the name of that country before. Recently.

Today, in fact.

"Weren't you just on the news an hour ago?"

"We met with your President's advisors this morning, so that is entirely possible."

Gabby simply stared. She tried to recall that random nanosec-ond she'd stopped to watch the dapper figures walking across the White House lawn on the television, just before she got in the shower.

Both men were tall dark and handsome. And they seemed older, though they didn't quite look it.

The king had a regal, East African handsomeness, but looked much too young to already be a king.

The vizier, Max, looked to be from another part of Africa. Perhaps Nigeria or Ghana. Tall even while he was sitting, and more built. He had a cleanly shaped goatee while the king was clean-shaven. His features were wide and full where the king's were sharp and tight, including his dark gleaming eyes. Unassuming but much more imposing.

The king stayed silent, donning a severe, intimidating look. Max continued with his disarming black stare, a vulnerability meant to put her at ease. He spoke with the coiled, hyphenated trill of the Middle East.

"We are here because we received news that the Princess Otieno, offspring of King Otieno, the former King of Ashwari, might be hiding in this country. And we believe you to be that offspring."

"Okay," Gabby simply replied.

"With your permission, we would like to test your DNA to make sure it is a match."

"It will match," Gabby assured them.

The king shifted in his chair, giving Max a look he was too busy watching her to return.

"If that is the case," Max nodded patiently, then the king has a proposition for you."

"The king doesn't speak for himself?" Gabby asked.

She could only imagine the horror on her mother's face behind her. Her father began reprimanding her in an Ashwari panic.

Gabby quietly took her rebuke, half turning to face him.

These were not her parents. They couldn't be her parents. The way they cowered so.

How had she missed it before today?

"...I'm sorry," Gabby muttered, remorsefully. The king spoke something in Arabic to Max and it dawned on her that the King may not even speak or understand English.

"The king is interested in forming an alliance between your country and his."

Forming an alliance?

With... Ashwari? With... America?

What the hell does that have to do with me? she thought

"I don't understand."

"Manaf is a prosperous country. Your father the King once sought an alliance with us, as well as his father before him."

"Is Manaf one of the countries that let him be murdered by traitors? And my mother as well?"

Max lowered his gaze and spoke in Arabic as if translating. The king replied in measured, commanding syllables.

"Your father's General lied to him, which in turn caused him to lie to my father," the king replied through Max. "As a result, my father was killed in his own palace by traitors, shortly after your family was assassinated."

Gabby swallowed, suddenly overwhelmed by the realities of countries outside the US.

"I still don't understand what this has to do with me."

"Your father and my father betrothed us to each other while we were very young," Max continued to translate. "If you are the rightful Queen of Ashwari as you yourself believe, then I propose a marriage between us. Between my country and yours."

Gabby shifted her weight on the arm of the couch, skimming

her fingers across her brow in thought.

"So... if I leave my family, my home, my profession behind, to go with you to... Monat, is it?"

"Manaf."

"Go with you to Manaf, and spend the rest of my life married to a strange man in a strange land, you promise to help a country that I have almost no connection to whatsoever, that's not even the size of Tampa?"

"*Asha!*"

"No, Mom, this is crazy," Gabby directed towards her. "Two Denzel lookin' dudes come to the door speaking Arabic, and suddenly you're willing to call me a queen and hand me off?"

The room was silent and Gabby sensed her parents' embarrassment.

She was starting to doubt her confidence, but the growing frustration over her puppeteered life needed expressing.

"I can understand my mother actually being a Queen, like... that's the only thing that you've ever told me that's made any sense," Gabby continued, "but let's just pretend for a moment that I believe you guys are who you say you are," she pointed with an outstretched arm. "I don't have a birth certificate, I don't have a green card or a visa, don't have a social security card, don't have a passport. And if I get caught leaving the country *without* it? I'll be deported anyway. So, until you somehow manage to get me one or *all* of those things, I'm gonna have real trouble entertaining any of this."

Max translated her rant in record time.

The king's high, sable cheekbones raised and his laugh lines appeared like strings, his mouth in a slight grin. He huffed a little laugh and addressed her directly.

"If I do this for you, do I have your hand in marriage?" he

asked in impeccable English.

Gabby shivered, feeling a bit sheepish. Every eye turned from the king's black eyes to Gabby's.

"I'll... think about it," Gabby squinted in disbelief. At the conversation, at the entire event.

The two men gave each other another wordless consultation that tonally seemed to amount to, "what choice do we have?"

Each of them raised from the table, the King giving her a nod as he headed for the door at a king's slow pace. Max followed behind, buttoning his camel trench as his Majesty walked out without a word.

"We will be in touch," Max faced the family with a slight bow.

"You must stay for dinner," Gabby's mother pleaded at the door. An Ashwari custom. Women of the house often pleaded for their guests to stay, whether they wanted them to or not, a familial sign of affection. In her case, she was probably serious.

"Another time," Max politely grinned with his eyes. Neither of them took a second look at Gabby on their way out.

The entire family crowded around the large living room window as the pair walked back to the black SUV parked on their curb.

Gabby tried to stave off curiosity, but eventually caved and looked through the peephole at their departure. The king's black coat floated in the wind as he got in on the driver's side.

At least he was the kind of king that was willing to drive himself around town. She liked that.

* * *

As the two men drove off back to their hotel in relative silence, the King finally caved.

"What?" the King asked, knowingly.

"Nothing," Mazigh shrugged.

"You obviously have something to add."

"You were charming."

"I hardly said a word," Khoury muttered.

"And it was charming," Mazigh insisted. "It seems the intel proved to be accurate," he broached the subject at hand.

The King let out a breath.

The information was exciting on its face. And then, there she was. Dressed like a commoner and making demands with complete confidence. She really was American.

But it suited her. Who she really was.

"Do you remember her mother?" the King asked.

"Vaguely. An Ethiopian woman. Also beautiful. She resembles her, no?"

He smoldered in thought. He remembered Ashwari's Queen through the words of others more than remembering what she looked like. Everyone went on about her poise and supermodel looks, down to her tall, athletic body type. The princess obviously inherited that, but she had her father's full lips and narrow eyes. And quite possibly his temperament.

"Perhaps. She certainly resembles the King."

"In more than just the physical," Mazigh smirked. "Shall I cancel the DNA kit?"

"Of course not. We'll need the proof," the King said.

"The girl has no country," Mazigh raised his eyebrows, a victorious smile on his face. "This will be easier than we anticipated. Extraction could be done in a matter of hours."

"Look into a visa for the girl."

Mazigh adopted a quizzical look. "What? Why?"

"Because her requests are reasonable."

"Not in the few days that we have."

"We must improvise," the King insisted. "We still need to conduct the exam and we need her compliance."

"...Or we could take her now, and conduct the exam at home. It would pose no risk. She is clearly the Princess."

"We stick to the plan," the King nodded. "Belkacem warned me of the obstacles."

"You rely on Belkacem too much," Mazigh offered. "Only one of us has ever set foot in America before today."

"And only one of us is King," Emir shot him a look of warning.

Mazigh breathed through his nose as he chose his next words carefully. "Time is of the essence. If we give in to her demands we will be at her mercy."

"We are at her mercy regardless," the King reasoned. "Her mother's friend has raised her well enough, but she has lived in fear of deportation. If I can grant her in a matter of days what her family hasn't been able to in a lifetime, she will come with us willingly."

"And if she looks you up on the internet in two days' time?"

Emir answered with the hope of a man accustomed to forcing circumstances to adjust to his needs. "Let us hope she does not."

"Eventually, she will find out the whole truth," Mazigh warned.

"Of course. Hopefully, the three of us will be on a plane by then."

His vizier's silence overwhelmed the King again.

"You have more to say, Mazigh?"

"Simply that there are potential wives all over Manaf, your majesty. Younger than 25."

"I want this one," was his loaded response.

"The likelihood that she is still a virgin—"

"She is of royal blood. Which is worth a thousand spotless virgins."

The silence of his vizier begged to differ, but he didn't dare speak another word. Besides, he knew the King well enough to know his wheels were turning.

Mazigh was not "old-fashioned." Marrying a virgin was simply the way of things. He would lose the respect of practically every man in Manaf if he did not.

He may be forgiven in this special circumstance. The King was positive that with her being raised across the world, he could keep her personal life under wraps. They stopped at a traffic light and a gentle rain started, pattering the windows.

"Find out what you can from the parents," he finally said.

"How would they know?"

"They would at least know her friends. Her social life."

"Everything about this evening tells me they probably haven't let the girl too far out of sight. She seems a bit sheltered, particularly for an American."

"We mustn't rely on our stereotypes. Find out for sure."

"Of course, your Majesty. And if she... has taken lovers?"

"She will have to be examined."

Mazigh's lips became tight as he shook his head. "She won't like that."

"Of course she won't."

"We can combine the DNA testing with the examination. Make it seem as arbitrary as possible," Mazigh suggested.

"I am now wondering whether I even want to know."

Mazigh gave him a nearly imperceptible smirk. "Only her attendants will truly need to know. Shall I keep his Majesty in the dark?"

"Please."

"Even if the results are pleasing?"

Mazigh knew him too well. That's what he gets for hiring his childhood friend to be his advisor.

The beautiful Princess Asha being a virgin was a longshot, but it would essentially make her perfect. Like a daydream. His own personal treasure that'd been hidden for him these senselessly hard, long twenty-five years. Waiting. Maturing.

Not that he'd entertained any women lately, but he'd held off for some reason after hearing the news. And now he knew why.

He wanted her. Like he had never wanted anything.

He'd born the burden of ruling a nation for most of his life, but he had never known want. He'd always had to experience it vicariously, through his friend.

Princess Asha was close enough to touch, but he couldn't. Not yet. The King dared to let his vizier observe his unmitigated thoughts.

"Especially if they are pleasing," he muttered, facing the rain-soaked window.

4

Chapter 4

Mackenzie sat cross-legged on her sister's bed that night, after their strange visitors had gone. An unfamiliar trap song played from Gabby's Webster app as she hugged one leg, with her chin resting on her knee in contemplative silence, looking at nothing.

It'd been a long time since her younger sister, who'd long ago filled out and matured far faster than Gabby, had come to her room to hang out. Knowing what she knew now, she didn't feel so insecure about that anymore. She used to think they shared the same eyes if nothing else, but that was apparently a coincidence. They sat for an awkward moment before finally, Mackenzie gathered the courage to speak.

"You do know that Mom's never going to speak to you again, right?" she raised an eyebrow.

"Why not?"

"You embarrassed her, talking to the freaking king of Manaf like that."

"You really think they were telling the truth?" Gabby wondered with a wrinkled brow.

"It'd be a strange thing to lie about," Mackenzie shrugged.

"Did *you* know who my parents were?"

"What? No," Mackenzie scoffed. "Who would tell me something like that?"

"You didn't suspect?"

"Not once. I mean... it seemed a little weird that you always seemed to have legal problems and we didn't. I just thought it was because you were darker."

Gabby looked at her sister for a moment before they burst into simultaneous giggles.

"It explains a lot, don't you think?" Gabby asked.

"What do you mean?"

"What do you mean, 'what do I mean'? I'm nothing like any of you guys."

"Yeah, our metabolism is terrible, and you're tall and gorgeous."

"I was gonna say that no one understands what I'm about and my boobs are non-existent," Gabby said dryly.

"You mean to tell me you really suspected we were never related because of *that*?"

"Faraj probably did," Gabby continued. "Always trying to tell me I was adopted."

"He told the same thing to me too."

Gabby looked around the room, surveying it. Even with a new paint job and IKEA furnishings she'd bought with her own money, it suddenly looked to her like a child's room. A child's room in a family's house she'd been squatting in. There wasn't a single thing in it she wanted to take with her.

And it was then that she realized that she'd already made her decision. She was going to get on a plane for the first time ever. With strangers.

"So I guess... this is goodbye, then," she sighed.

Mackenzie knit her brow anxiously. "Surely not yet."

"Not yet, but soon. If he's really a king, he won't stay here forever."

"What are you gonna do about school?"

Gabby's stomach jolted because she'd genuinely forgotten. School. The nursing home. Mrs. Holderman.

Gabby started to get emotional. She had a life here. People who counted on her were in it. And if she were truly the rightful Queen of Ashwari, how her responsibilities have multiplied. A small seed of readiness seemed to sprout in her being.

"I guess... I guess that's over now," she shrugged, her lip trembling. Mackenzie's eyes glistened but Gabby's tears fell faster than she could wipe them, surprised at her little sister's emotion. Mackenzie could be moody, but she hardly ever cried.

"One hell of a promotion, though," Mackenzie sniffed.

"That part," Gabby giggled, wiping her eyes.

"You don't seem very excited."

"I am, but... I've never had to be responsible for anything, except for my chores. You see how long it took for Mom to let me have a car."

"I'm sure the King knows a thing or two," her sister snickered. "You won't be doing it alone. He just needs you to look fierce on his arm anyway."

"You seem more excited than me," Gabby noticed. "Can't wait to get rid of me, huh?"

"It's gonna be weird as hell when you leave," her sister moaned, laying on her folded arms. "But the more we talk about it... it's so obvious that this is your destiny, Gabby. So yeah. I'm beyond excited for you."

Gabby smirked against her will as her thoughts went to the

king. "What'd you think of him?" she asked with a wrinkled nose.

"Who, the King?"

"Yeah. I mean, he didn't talk much but he seemed a little like... I don't know. He wasn't exactly a barrel of laughs."

"No, but he's hot. All king-like and... manly," Mackenzie confessed without reservation.

"Definitely a lot of manliness in our dining room today," Gabby muttered, looking far off in contemplation as she pinched her bottom lip with a thumb and forefinger.

If she marries the King, that probably meant he would want everything that went along with it. Including babies. And how they're made. Her sex twitched involuntarily.

"The foreign languages thing is hot," her sister volunteered.

"Yep."

"Smelled like wealth."

"Mm-hm," Gabby hummed, hypnotized.

"How much you wanna bet he's cut to death under those clothes?"

"What about the other one?" Gabby squinted.

Mackenzie rolled her eyes and scoffed. "Gabby, no," she whined.

"What?"

"Don't come up with ways to be contrary."

"I'm not!"

"You can't fall for the right-hand man, so don't even think about it," Mackenzie warned.

Gabby laughed. "They're *both* highly fuckable, okay? I'm allowed to admit that."

"Gabby, *noooo*," her sister groaned again.

"C'mon, you know I love a number two guy."

35

"Just... stop yourself right now."

"I know, I know."

"Don't just say 'I know.' This is the King of a *middle east* country, girl. You are gonna get that man fired. Or *killed*, playin' around."

"I would never do that. Besides, I don't even know him, but you know what? I just learned a valuable ass thing about myself today."

"What's that?"

"Everyone always told me I was too picky. But I just agreed to marry a stranger. In exchange for my citizenship." Gabby's mouth drew downward at the corners as she shrugged. "I didn't think twice about it. I think I know why I've never had a boyfriend, or never cared that I didn't get to go to all the proms. Spring Break." Gabby nodded with a far-off look, unspoken confirmation in her tone. "I think I might for real be stuck up."

Mackenzie didn't even try to talk her out of it.

"Yeah, but... in a good way," she defended.

"Don't try to make it not be messy," Gabby rolled her eyes.

"No, seriously," Mackenzie raised up on her elbows, insistent that her sister understood this about herself. "You agreed to marry him if he *delivered*, there's a difference."

"It's like, as soon as he said the word 'duty' it was like I came alive," Gabby admitted.

"He never said the word 'duty,' I don't think."

"You know what I mean, Kenzie," Gabby tossed her head. "If this guy is for real... if he's really the King and I'm really a Queen, I mean... maybe I'll never feel those butterflies in my stomach when he's near me... ever. But still. I'm not sure that even exists."

"It does," Mackenzie ignored her.

"I'd be an idiot to pass this up. Wouldn't I?"

Mackenzie drew in a big breath before she continued. "Well, I'm glad that's you're attitude. Because I have a feeling you might not really have a choice.

"Kenzie, he might be the King of Manaf, but I'm still the Queen of Ashwari," Gabby retorted. "He can't make me do *shit*."

"Okay, Miss Queen," her sister returned the sass. "But your country is effed up right now. You need his help."

Gabby blinked from curled up position as she stared at her bedspread. "Maybe the U.S. would help."

Mackenzie lowered her head, but her eyes didn't move. "Gabby. America doesn't even know who you are. This guy does. This guy found you when no one else *could*. This guy traveled day and night to get here, because you're *valuable* to him."

Her sister's words caused Gabby's whole body to stir. She couldn't stop her mouth muscles forming into a smile.

Hmm. Valuable, huh?

"C'mon, Sis," Gabby suddenly bounded from her bed and reached for the laptop on her desk. "Think it's time you and me did a little research."

* * *

"Last pill, Mrs. Holderman," Gabby was sing-songing the very next day.

"Okay, honey," Mrs. Holderman lilted in her quakey southern drawl.

Mrs. Holderman was back to her polite, lovely self when Gabby returned to her work-study as usual. Her roommate had fallen in the night and was moved out of the convalescent wing to hospice.

Mrs. Holderman seemed to be blissfully unaware that she ever even had a roommate today. In her mind, Gabby pondered a link between Mrs. Holderman's behavior and the absence of her roommate.

Gabby may have found out last night that she's technically the Queen of Ashwari, but explain that to the Sunnyside Nursing Home scheduling manager.

She hadn't seen or heard from the mysterious men since last night, and it made her realize how vulnerable she was to swindlers. Anyone, really, but especially her.

Last night, two men just waltzed into their house with a whole royal dog and pony show and it caused her parents to come clean about her true identity.

No one thought to ask for I.D., contact information, or even ask themselves what the proper protocol is for kings showing up at one's house in the middle of the afternoon unannounced.

She didn't realize how dumb it all was until life went back to usual the next morning. She didn't realize how much she'd wanted it until there was no word of them in 18 hours.

"You alright?" Sara asked as they straightened up the newly vacant bed.

"Yeah, just... distracted," Gabby replied, smoothing wrinkles absent-mindedly out of the sheets.

"You sure?"

"Yeah, yeah I'll be fine."

"Gabby?" the floor manager's voice startled them from the doorway.

"Yes ma'am?"

"There's a gentleman out here to see you. A... Max? He's saying he's here to pick you up."

"Oh geez," Gabby sighed, more from the adrenaline coursing

through her. Well, at least it wasn't all a dream.

"Gabby, you tryin' to keep your girl in the dark??" Sara protested as Gabby made her way around the other side of the bed and out of the room.

"You know you have to put in a request at least two weeks in advance if you're needing time off," the floor manager tensely reminded her.

"I'm not," Gabby stuttered. "I mean... I'll handle it."

Gabby ignored the eyes as she headed downstairs and across the hall to the entrance of the facility.

Lo and behold, a tall, square-shouldered man that could only be Max from behind, towered elegantly over Brenda at the receptionist desk in a white dress shirt and slacks, filling the front area with his exotic scent.

Brenda was clearly overwhelmed, trying to ignore his direct stare boring through her. She was too intimidated even to make small talk. He wasn't trying to be intimidating. He certainly wasn't flirting. He was just unequivocally not from the West.

When Brenda made curious eye contact with Gabby still a ways off, Max whirled around to face her with a slight bow, a reverent smile in his eyes.

Gabby's heart did a little flip.

She told herself it was the situation and not the man. The fact that this was all still real.

Her sister was right. She can't start off entertaining this thing with the vizier. Gabby didn't utter a word until they were eye to eye in front of each other.

"What are you doing here?" Gabby quietly inquired.

"I stopped by your house this morning to have a conversation with your mother, who was most helpful. She said you left for work this morning."

"Well, I couldn't very well stop my life," Gabby explained. "For all I know, this could all be some elaborate scam."

"Scam?"

"Yeah. You all could be human traffickers for all I know."

Max stared as if he had no concept of jokes.

"You have an appointment. At Sinai Community Health Center," he said.

"When?"

"Now."

"My appointment is scheduled for 'now o'clock,' is that it?" Gabby raised her eyebrows.

"Yes, my Queen."

"I'm not your Queen," she corrected. "Not yet, anyway."

"Not of Manaf, no. But you are still Queen of Ashwari by blood, your Majesty."

"Oh Lord, can you please keep your voice down?" Gabby mumbled.

"Of course," he replied, at the exact same volume.

"Wait here. I only have about two patients left, I just need to talk to my supervisor and the other nurse on duty."

Max suddenly registered her all-white uniform. "You're a nurse here?"

"Yes. Well, in training."

"Your birth mother was a nurse. Before she became Queen."

Gabby's eyes sparkled. "...Really?"

"So the story goes. Your parents never told you?"

For some reason the question made her feel embarrassed.

"No, I mean... they never talked about..."

Before Gabby could finish, Gabby's supervisor was coming down the hallway.

"Miss Ayenew? You've left Sara out in the lurch, upstairs."

"Ms. Martin," Gabby startled.

"Everything okay?"

Max interjected forcefully. "Miss Ayenew has a family emergency. She will be leaving work today."

Ms. Martin just looked gobsmacked at Max. She couldn't think of a thing to say to the dark dashing stranger that'd inserted himself into an employee conversation.

"Max, let me handle this."

"Who's this?" Ms. Martin asked.

"This is... my... cousin," Gabby lied. "Max. He's visiting. From Manaf."

"How do you do," Max half-bowed.

"Manaf. Where on Earth is that?"

"It borders Ghassan, just off the coast of the Arabian Sea."

"Oh," Ms. Martin's voice went up in recognition, "the MeTv guy's country."

"Correct," Max smiled.

"Have you ever met him?"

"...He's a very good friend of the King's," Max measured his words.

"Oh, you know, those royals, I'm sure they hang out all the time," Gabby tried to grab the reigns of her lie. "Nothing like *our* family, right *Max?*"

"Right," nodded Max.

The distraction, though pleasant, was wildly against protocol. Ms. Martin turned toward Gabby with a stern but gracious look that was saying, "*you're doing great but leave your family members at home.*"

"Sara's got Mr. Peterson. Just do Dr. Haber and you're done for the day," she ordered.

"Will do."

"What about tomorrow?" Ms. Martin asked.

"I'm off tomorrow."

"What about Thursday?"

"She will keep you posted," Max chimed in. Gabby nodded awkwardly, hoping Ms. Martin was just focusing on how professional she had been up until today.

"Okay. Go."

Gabby turned quietly to Max, deciding to forego explaining his presence altogether. "I'll be about ten minutes."

"Very well," he said, watching her disappear down the hall. Ms. Martin stood there awkwardly, suddenly unable to excuse herself from his presence.

This man was somehow as manly as her grandfather, and yet he was at least a decade younger than she was. She was just about to tell him it was against policy for him to be there if he wasn't there to visit someone.

"Your receptionist tells me you have a resident here from Manaf," he mentioned.

Ms. Martin could only stare like a deer in headlights.

"Mrs. Nader," Brenda filled in behind her.

"Oh, yes!"

"Would it be possible to visit with her?"

Ms. Martin looked back at Brenda who was already grinning like a Cheshire cat.

"I... think it would thrill her in the extreme. Actually," said Ms. Martin, charmed.

* * *

Meanwhile, upstairs Gabby was just finishing up in Dr. Haber's room. She heard a commotion downstairs growing to a swell and she stopped folding sheets for a moment just to make sure she wasn't hallucinating. Nursing homes weren't exactly teeming with activity in the afternoons.

Sara peeked her head in just as Gabby was putting away Dr. Haber's medicine.

"What's going on down there?" Gabby asked.

"Your fine ass cousin is talking to Mrs. Nader downstairs."

"How'd you know he was my cousin?"

"Girl, please, everybody knows. Nobody on the first floor is even working anymore."

Gabby made it back downstairs where a crowd had gathered around Mrs. Nader's door.

The crowd of staff parted to let Gabby see inside her room, where Max was carrying on a lively conversation in an unknown language.

"How come you never told us you were from Manaf?" Sara elbowed her.

"Probably because I'm not," Gabby whispered.

"Isn't he your cousin?"

"He is. He's... my... cousin by marriage."

"What's he doing here?"

"Family emergency."

"No, I mean, what's he doing in Mrs. Nader's room?"

"Your cousin asked to speak to her," Mrs. Nader's nurse answered them both.

"Speak to Mrs. Nader?"

The nurse nodded, distracted as she watched them. "Brenda told him she was from Manaf."

"I thought Mrs. Nader was non-verbal?" wondered Sara with a knitted brow.

Her Puerto Rican nurse waved a hand with a suck of her teeth.

"She only pretended to be so that she wouldn't be bothered."

When Gabby entered the doorway, Max pointed with a smile, one that nearly melted Gabby on the spot.

Meanwhile, Mrs. Nader's face lit up like a Christmas tree as she beckoned Gabby to come forward. Gabby bent down in front of the weathered old woman and let her press Gabby's cheeks together with her hands and heartfelt laughter. She said the same unknown phrase again and again. Before long, a smile was plastered on Gabby's face also.

"What's she saying?" Gabby turned to him.

"Not here. Later," he said with a slight head shake.

Mrs. Nader took hold of Max's face in the same manner with a kiss to his head. Anyone religious or otherwise could see she was clearly blessing him. He got up respectfully from his chair next to her bed.

"Shall we?" he suddenly asked.

Gabby gave him a befuddled expression as she shook her head and scoffed.

"I'm ready when you are," she chirped.

5

Chapter 5

"Should I follow you?" Gabby asked.

"Follow me?"

"In my car."

Max looked over at the beat-up old coupe in the parking lot, the same one that was in the driveway in front of her house last night.

"We'll pick it up after," he said.

Gabby held herself by the arms with a slight look of hesitation as they slowly approached the familiar black SUV. His rental car alone was nicer than any car she'd ever driven in. She took a mental note of the license plate, in case they were the most distinguished set of kidnappers in Tampa.

"Okay, what was that back there?" Gabby asked as Max opened the passenger side door and the new car smell wafted out.

"What was what?"

"Mrs. Nader. I've never seen her so responsive this entire semester. What were you doing in there?"

"She spotted me from the hallway and greeted me in the Manaf tradition," he said as if that were commonplace. Gabby stared and stared.

"When??"

"You had already gone."

"She's from Jamaica, Queens," Gabby said with a squint of suspicion.

"She told me she left Manaf as a girl. She had a message for the King."

"I see," she raised her eyebrows, surprised. "And what was it?"

"Confidential, I'm afraid." With the push of a button, Max smoothly started up the plush vehicle.

"Did you tell her the truth? About me?"

"I may have divulged a secret or two," Max grinned.

"The two of you are terrible at espionage, you know that?" Gabby giggled. She wanted the middle armrest but the manspread was overwhelming. She drew her hands to her lap.

"She asked me what I was doing there. Only a heartless man would lie," he added.

"What *you* were doing there? How does she know who *you* are?"

"...She didn't," he responded cryptically. Gabby looked out the window of the smooth driving SUV, the GPS system spouting out directions. He backed out of the parking lot and they were on their way.

"Will you really deliver Mrs. Nader's message to him?"

"Of course."

"You should have the King come by. She'd probably get up and dance."

"Perhaps. If we have time."

Gabby was feeling electric with Max next to her, and she wondered how long it would take for either of them to figure out she was a complete and total noob.

Being around boys that hadn't been bribed by her parents to come over short-circuited her bad enough. Being in the same room with the King again, knowing full well who he was now, was sure to fold her in knots.

She supposed this would soon be her regular life. It was quite nice having a Max around. All polite and dutiful and trustworthy. She wondered if he would serve them both or if she would get a girl version. Probably the latter.

So far everything looked familiar as it whizzed by Gabby's passenger window. Wherever they were going seemed to be in the neighborhood.

"Will I be seeing the King today?"

"Would you like to?" wondered Max, like a computer program.

"Would he like to see me?" she wondered back.

Max looked over at her as he raised one eyebrow and grinned.

Gabby swallowed. "I just mean... if I'm going to be marrying him I should probably, you know, talk to him," Gabby backpedaled, suddenly shy.

"There will be plenty of time to get acquainted once we get back to Manaf. Time is of the essence, you understand."

Geez. Is this really fucking happening? As soon as the results come back, she's off?

"Sure, but... doesn't King Khoury want to get to know me?"

"You must refer to him as 'the King' or 'his Majesty.'"

Gabby jerked her neck back a bit. "Even once we're... married?"

"You may refer to him as 'husband' in private. But you should

47

refrain from using his given name."

Did he mean his first name?

"Emir?"

Max visibly stiffened. "Where did you learn that?"

"The internet. And also you told me it. Yesterday."

Max paused. "Like I said. You should refrain from using the King's given name. I will use the short time we have here to instruct you in all the ways a queen is expected to act. Once you leave America, liberties will not be allowed to be taken."

Gabby faced forward, suddenly acquiring a distaste for protocols. "You assume I'm leaving with you," she said.

"The Queen agreed to return with us to Manaf."

"On the condition that you can get me American citizenship."

Since they were at the stoplight, Max reached behind them for a manila envelope in the backseat and placed it in Gabby's lap.

Gabby looked down at the weighty packet. No way.

She cocked her head suspiciously as she pinched the tabs and reached in to grab the thick stack of paperwork inside. The sight of a letter with an embossed American seal embedded in the middle greeted her. And it had her name on it.

"What is this?" she asked, glancing over as he drove.

"Your papers," he answered stoically.

"I don't believe you," she said in fervent disbelief, eagerly digging through the envelope's contents.

"Obviously it was expedited," he filled in as she dumped it all like a Christmas present. "It wasn't easy, but it also wasn't as difficult as we anticipated. Your president has been accommodating."

"It hasn't even been 24 hours."

"The King called on his 'royal friend' in Ghassan for help," Max said, referring to Bel.

"I can't believe you know the MeTv guy," she mused as she emptied the rest of the envelope and a little blue booklet fell out.

A Welcome to U.S.A. Citizenship.

"Is this real?"

She saw an official-looking letter. *Your Visa Application has been approved*, it read. She stared and stared at it until her eyes blurred with tears. A hand covered the bottom half of her face.

"Not quite a green card but it is a start," Max said. Gabby didn't know what to say.

"Oh my God."

"The Princess is pleased," Max cheerfully concluded.

"Do you know what this means, Max?" she gushed, her palpable joy filling the front seat.

"What does it mean," he grinned, his eyes on the road.

"It means I'm free," she sniffed, looking out of the windshield with new eyes. "I was free all morning and I didn't even know. I can breathe," she exhaled, as if testing it out. "I can plan for the future now. I can build something without fear that I'll be arrested and lose it all."

Max stayed quiet as she continued to peruse the paperwork in reverence. A pang of guilt shot through him.

"I'm afraid you only have two days of American freedom to experience."

"That's okay," she sighed with a smile. "That's okay. Before the King arrived, I didn't have any."

The SUV pulled up to a small clinic. Gabby hopped out of the vehicle in good spirits.

"My Queen. You will have to remember to stay put until someone attends to you."

"Gotta be honest, I can't even imagine that," Gabby replied making her way to the front door. Max rushed to get there first to open it.

They were greeted by a front lobby emptied of patients and the staff that was standing in a line, from shortest to tallest. Gabby raised an eyebrow.

She'd only ever gone to clinics, even if she was deathly ill (which was not allowed in her house), but she was pretty sure that folks with insurance didn't usually get this kind of service.

"Lemme guess," Gabby smiled, "you all are also from Manaf?"

"Yes, my Queen," one of them smiled. "Dr. Aikende is actually from Ashwari. He will do your examination today."

"No kidding!" Gabby replied, surprised. There was a close-knit community of Ashwari that lived in Tampa. Incredibly small. She would've remembered if there was a doctor.

"Yes, my Queen," another one of them nodded.

"Well technically, I guess I *am* his queen. I don't know, we'll see, right?"

The staff just stood there smiling giddily.

"This is, uh, Max. The king's vizier," Gabby gestured. The introduction garnered giggles from the staff.

One of them spoke in perfect English. "We're already acquainted with the… Max. My Queen."

"We spoke earlier. They were kind enough to let us use their facilities this afternoon," Max filled in.

"Well, a girl could get used to this 'no wait times' thing," Gabby joked. The staff gave her a hearty laugh that seemed genuine enough, so she kept going. "If the test comes out negative, keep it to yourself."

"This way, your Majesty," a short, middle eastern woman directed with a short bow.

She led Gabby down a long corridor that betrayed the clinic's diminutive size from the outside. Exam tables, scales, and computers sat in the middle of the large corridor lined on each side with doors open to empty exam rooms. She stopped at a room at the end of the hallway on the left, exam room 3.

"Get undressed if you would, please. The doctor will be in shortly."

Undressed?? To draw blood?

As the door latched closed behind her, Gabby looked around the room. The posters on the wall, all about women's health, STD's, and vaginas, let her know she was definitely at a gynecologist's office.

Were they testing her for diseases? Pregnancy?

Finally, she understood and she snickered, shaking her head.

Jesus. The one time her virginity has ever come in handy. If she could even put it that way.

Granted, he was a King and all. Naturally, he would want "a fresh one."

And she was a stranger to him. Other than the home advantage, his life would be changing just as much as hers.

Still. She was relying on her Wikipedia knowledge and having the MeTV founder as her neighbor to save her. It was still a different culture. Just what was she getting herself into?

Not a moment later there was a knock on the door. Another black man in a lab coat walked in, followed by the nurse from the hallway. She shut the door behind them.

"Miss... Ayenew, is it?" the doctor began.

"That's what they say."

"I'm Dr. Aikende. I'll be doing your examination today."

"What examination am I here to have done, exactly?" Gabby inquired.

The nurse gave the doctor a look he didn't return, which

confirmed her suspicions.

"We'll be doing blood work today, screen for diseases, cancer cells," Dr. Aikende answered tactfully. 'The King has ordered all labs be done on you."

"This all seems a little... unorthodox, Doctor," Gabby pressed. "I'm in nursing school right now, did the King mention that?"

"He did not," he replied, with an upward tone of interest.

"I've had a gynecological exam in the last year. I've been tested for HPV. If it's medical records they want, I could give it to them."

"The King trusts the results from his own resources, as you can imagine," he explained. *Good answer*, she thought.

"Lie back for me," he said.

Soooo, Dr. Aikende was about to look at his Majesty's snatch, no big deal. Someone has to do it, right? She looked over at the "drink plenty of water" poster in silence, one arm over her head.

She sighed. Gabby wasn't sensing any red flags, but things definitely weren't as they seemed. She wanted to go with them, so she wasn't sure what all the secrecy was about. It made things that should be innocuous suspicious.

"You're going to feel something cold here."

"Do you think I'm the Princess, Doctor?" Gabby blurted, suddenly craving transparency.

"It's highly probable, yes," he readily offered.

His words encouraged her. "Why is that?"

"Aside from your obvious resemblance, I remember the Queen's visit to America very well."

He was talking about her mother. She suddenly felt warmth when someone mentioned her.

"You were here?"

"I was in Ashwari at the time," he divulged as he worked. "I wouldn't flee the country for a few more years. Queen Aida was the reason I moved to Florida."

The pressure down below reminded Gabby where she was. She tried to focus.

"So you were there. When the rebellion broke out."

"I was, my Queen."

She didn't know much about the politics of Ashwari, but she knew about the rebellion. Everyone in her small ex-pat community did. As much as they didn't like talking about it, it was brought up an awful lot. If she knew it involved her parents, she would've listened more carefully.

"...What happened?" Tentatively she asked, afraid he may not want to recall. The doctor kept his head down, eyes on his work.

He was quiet a moment as if searching his compassion. He imagined to be so ignorant of one's own identity, it would follow she would be just as ignorant about her country.

"Your father's General staged a coup," he slowly exhaled. "It took us all by surprise, but.... looking back it was inevitable. There was a lot of unrest among the young people, who felt your father was simply a puppet for the surrounding allies." Gabby heard him fiddling with instruments on a metal tray. Probably the depressor.

"King Otieno was notoriously corrupt and paranoid. We had to beg for every resource. General Olayinka seemed like he would make a good leader. But then... the slaughter began."

"Of my family?" she deduced.

"Of everyone, but yes, of your family."

"Of everyone but me," she said in a firm tone. The nurse was deathly quiet.

"It looks that way."

"Do you know if they... were they made to suffer?"

The doctor sighed a sigh, reluctant to be the person to do both this job and that one.

"It's a bit gruesome, your Majesty. Has the King not answered your questions?"

"I only just met him yesterday. Briefly, at that," Gabby explained, trying on a more queenly air. "If it's painful for you to recall, then forget I asked."

"I'm only thinking of you, Princess."

"Then don't worry about me. I'm a big girl, I can take it."

The pressure between her legs abruptly left. The doctor handed the nurse several swabs and she turned to put them in vials.

"The family was beheaded and hung outside the palace gates," he recounted matter-of-factly. "Including a small infant girl who was presumed to be you."

Gabby's breath caught. The doctor had been right to be prudent.

For some reason, her sympathies bypassed her parents altogether and rested solely on the little girl. Who was she?

"You may sit up. We're all done, your Majesty," his nurse chimed in.

Gabby slowly sat up, clutching her paper gown where it loosened in the back. "May I have your honest opinion?"

"Of course," the doctor nodded.

"Do you believe these men are who they say they are?"

He laughed a little as if what she'd asked was quaint. "I know they are, my Queen."

"Do *you* think it's a good idea for me to go back?" Gabby sought his unbiased counsel.

The doctor stood and disposed of his gloves in the nearby trash can. "I wouldn't agree to do this if I didn't. Even if you weren't

King Otieno's daughter, but I believe you are. And if the people can believe, they can have hope. Knowing you're alive would give us all a hope we didn't think we'd ever know again. And Manaf is a strong ally."

Gabby swallowed and then launched into another question before she could stop herself. "What if I'm not good enough?"

The doctor stopped for a moment as if her question warranted the extra consideration.

"The fact that you are willing to sacrifice your life in America to save your country is proof enough that you are good enough."

Gabby left out the bit about being an illegal alien for the moment. It wasn't much of a sacrifice when her time in America was all borrowed anyway.

The doctor made his way to the door as he spoke softly to the nurse. He turned to Gabby and nodded toward her clothes, his next words loaded with meaning.

"Come. Your King awaits."

6

Chapter 6

Max waited patiently just outside the exam room, his stomach in bubbles.

Everything was going according to plan. Better, in fact. The fact that they found a Manafi run clinic with an Ashwari doctor, in the same city as the Princess, was a bonafide sign from God.

This was going to work out. He was a mess of urgency, excitement, and unplaced dread.

This was going to be good for Manaf. Good for the Khoury line.

The King was in love with her. He knew without a word being spoken between them. He'd followed that golden gut of his and it hadn't failed him yet.

So why did Max still feel like something bad was going to happen?

Perhaps it was guilt over giving the Princess fake immigration papers.

He couldn't have regretted his visual aids idea more than he had watching her openly fawn all over them.

48 hours suddenly seemed unbearably long. Long enough for more things to backfire.

Perhaps it was simply because the King had never experienced a single good thing before today, only had made the most of terrible things. His heart ached.

Midway through his thoughts, the doctor emerged.

"Doctor? How did she do?"

"Fine. The results will take some time."

"More than a day?"

"No, sir. Come back in two hours. They will be ready."

Max stood, his significant stature overpowering that of the doctor's. "I appreciate your discretion in this matter, Doctor."

"It was truly an honor," Dr. Aikende replied as the two men shook hands. Max gave his shoulder a firm squeeze. A moment later Gabby emerged from the exam room fully dressed.

"Ready?" she asked.

"Yes, Princess."

Gabby got a taste of the royal life as they again greeted all the staff on the way out. Max opened the passenger side door of the SUV for Gabby to enter.

"Do they drive on the same side of the street in Manaf?"

"They do, Princess."

"Oh. Good." Max slowly began closing the door and Gabby stopped it with her hand.

"I would like to see the King. Today," she suddenly said, before Max closed her in.

He remained silent, shutting her door and waiting until he'd made his way to the driver seat.

"May I ask why?" he said, starting the engine.

"Because I would like to speak with him."

"About?"

Gabby was losing patience. Did they have a sympathetic bone in their bodies?

"I just... I feel like I'm completely alone in this and I need him to put me at ease about this entire process," she explained in a short tone. "Because I am close to freaking out."

"'Freaking out?'" Max quoted.

"Yes! I'm being moved along a non-specified schedule here and there to marry a king that everyone keeps hiding from me, for some reason."

Max slowly backed out of the parking lot before continuing. Why Max expertly operating a car seemed so impressive to her she couldn't pinpoint.

"My Queen, as you well know, this is a sensitive mission," Max said, clearly placating her.

"Yes, yes, you keep saying that. My entire life is about to change drastically, and no one seems to care. Least of all the King. Almost as if the two of you were stringing me along."

She already smelled bullshit. But then let him know her trust was still there, for now. Max could only think about what a respectable, measured queen she would make.

"I assure you, the King has put the priority of your safety above his own. Has nothing you've witnessed today convinced you?"

Gabby had to admit it had. She supposed he could've hired all those people at the Dr.'s office, but no way had he paid off Mrs. Nader to turn in *that* performance.

"Well, as trustworthy as you seem to be, Max, I'd rather hear it from him."

"Of course, Princess," Max conceded. "But I will have to supervise."

"Fine with me. I'm not particularly jazzed to be alone with

this guy," she said, looking out the window as they stopped at a light.

Her response caught him off guard. "No?"

"No," she repeated.

His curiosity won out almost immediately. "Why not?"

Gabby huffed a giggle at his clueless question. "Because he's a stranger? That I seem to know less and less about, the more I find out?"

"Find out? From whom?"

"From you. From a little thing called a search engine."

Max put on a voice of casual curiosity. "And what in your research compels you to feel this way?"

"You seem awfully curious, Max."

"As the closest person to him, I'd be interested to... compare notes," Max explained.

"Well. As I said, I didn't seem to find out much. In fact, I didn't know what to believe. Is it true that he's been the king since he was eight???"

"That is true."

"I simply can't fathom that," Gabby lowered her voice, as though gossiping. "All that responsibility at eight."

"Children grow up faster in Manaf than they do in America. Duty was instilled in him from infancy as the Prince," Max reasoned, emotionless.

"Yeah, but... as grown up as I ever tried to be as a kid, my childlike grasp of things was always cringey in hindsight."

Max spat out another rebuttal as though a computer. "The king has always been dogmatic, moreso as a child. I am sure he regrets some of his early decisions. But every king must grow into his role. King Khoury's was simply... more literal."

Gabby noticed Max was moving without the GPS this time.

Had he already learned his way around??

"Surely he had advisors."

"He had his father's entire cabinet killed when he became king."

Whoa pump the brakes, she thought.

"Why?"

"Was it not in your research?"

That King Khoury was Robin from the Eyrie? No, it wasn't.

"All it said was that his father was assassinated in the palace and that he assumed the throne when he was eight."

Max hmphed. "Too gruesome for the textbooks, I imagine," he cynically replied.

"Where were *you* during all this?" the Princess wondered. Max was touched that she would even ask.

"I was a child. Growing up in a coastal village. My parents were both teachers."

"How did you come to be in the King's service?"

"The King wished to be educated in history and religion. My father was appointed him."

"Lucky teacher."

"Indeed."

"You grew up in the palace?"

"My father lived in the palace several years, sending home his salary. After that, the King sent for us all."

"*I* see," Gabby nodded her head slowly, starting to get a full picture. "And the King gained a playmate, as well."

"As much as a king can be played with," Max tempered. "I did, however, introduce him to pranks."

"What kind of pranks?" Gabby giggled.

"We often dressed alike and tried to fool the servants."

Gabby smiled until her cheeks hurt trying to imagine Max as

a boy playing pranks.

"And how successful were you at that?"

"Surprisingly, not very."

Gabby laughed. "Surprisingly huh? You'd have to be blind to work for the King every day and not be able to recognize him, I think. Besides, the two of you look nothing alike."

"You don't think so?"

"No. Related perhaps, but certainly not the same person."

"Every ten-year-old boy looks relatively the same to everyone except his mother," Max reasoned. "I sometimes pretended to be him on diplomatic errands to meet with foreign leaders, and he me."

"Sounds... dangerous."

"It was, but I had no sense of that," Max recalled. "It was great fun for me. The inevitable reveal was always priceless. An hour of anonymity was sometimes all the King desired."

"What a blessing for him," was Gabby's choice of words.

Max kept quiet, suddenly overcome with warm emotions.

In truth, the King had become his brother, an unassuming arrow in his quiver, an unexpected joy in the midst of horror. He wanted to smile at her observation. He supposed he could've, but thought it inappropriate somehow.

"It was. A blessing."

"The two of you are quite close, then."

"Indeed."

Gabby was quiet the rest of the way as the smooth ride of the SUV took them back to the nursing home where her car was parked.

"So, are we agreed?"

Max sighed in surrender. "You have a day off tomorrow, correct?"

"Yes."

"Very well," he nodded. "I will pick you up at your home tomorrow, and I will take you to see the king."

"I said I wanted to see the King today," Gabby replied in a soft but firm tone.

Max shook his head resolutely. "The king will need time to prepare."

"For what?" Gabby badgered. Max took a deep breath as if to temper his exasperation.

"It is not part of our custom that the bride see the King so frequently before they are married. But I understand that this is an extraordinary circumstance."

"The King never sees the Bride?" Gabby furrowed her brow. "How do they get to know each other? How does the King even shoot his shot?"

"Explain the term, 'shoot his shot.'"

Adorable. Gabby found herself blushing.

"Like... approaching a woman for a date," Gabby grinned. "How does the King approach a woman if he's never in the same room with her?"

"A king does not 'shoot his shot' in Manaf. Or anywhere," Max replied as if offended. "He is a king. He selects a wife, and the wife becomes Queen."

"He doesn't even want to have a conversation with her?"

"Perhaps. But conversations have no bearing in a king's decision to marry."

"I see," Gabby's tone turned defensive. "Because the Queen, as a rule, won't be doing that much talking?"

"The Queen may speak to her own contentment."

Gabby burst into laughter. "How progressive of you!"

"A king knows what he wants. Especially his majesty King

Khoury. He came all this way without ever having had a conversation with you."

This point was becoming more and more suspicious the more it was brought up.

"So he doesn't care about me beyond the political gains of marrying me," Gabby deduced.

Max thought for a moment, choosing his words carefully. Telling her about the King's emotions upon first seeing her would simply embolden her further.

"His mother was also from Ashwari, so there is sentiment behind his decision as well," he divulged instead.

The insight made her feel better, oddly. To know that there was a heart in there that was emotionally invested in her and the country she was leaving everything behind to save.

"I think you are concerned with romance," Max aggressively cut through her thoughts.

Gabby remained motionless, fearful that she would give something away that even she didn't know about.

"It's romance to have a conversation?"

"You wish to have a courtship ritual."

Heat rose to her cheeks against her will. Max talked like an alien and had the good looks of an alien. One that had procured a perfect male specimen to inhabit. Based on the research of female arousal and fertility cycles.

"I'm just saying, I'd like to talk to him. To reach an understanding. I'm still the Queen of Ashwari, if everyone's behavior around me is any indication. I'm not some peasant girl waiting for my lucky break to marry a king. Does a king's selection usually have as much leverage as I do?"

"Not usually. And for this very reason," Max had no trouble saying. "A king's obligations are strenuous. The last thing he needs is to be subject to the ministrations of a girl who has only learned she is Queen in the last 24 hours."

Uh... okay, what? She gave Max a wordless neck jerk.

"Ministrations? You misunderstand me, Max."

"I don't think so," he steadily asserted. "I have heard you refer to this power you wield on several occasions to get what you want."

Gabby slowly turned to face him in her seat, her brow furrowed in frustration as she struggled to keep her voice calm.

"What choice do I have?" she asked. "I'm about to leave everything I know behind to go to the other side of the world and be some stranger's *wife*. I'm practically being kidnapped. I'm just asking for some sympathy."

"King al Malwali was right about American women," he muttered, almost to himself. "In what other country would marrying a king garner this much protest?"

"Protest? I just want a conversation!" she exclaimed in awe.

"For now. And we've barely begun."

Gabby froze as she studied Max's sleepy expression that, thankfully, didn't seem to be malicious. Just arrogant. And, unfortunately, sexy.

It was not the greatest sign that she wasn't in for a machismo shit show. For that insight alone, was she glad to be having this conversation now rather than later.

"I need to speak to him now, more than ever. Because I have to believe that you don't represent him in this."

"I know the King's mind. And he would side with me."

"Well then, the King's pride is more fragile than it has any right to be. Has he ever been to any other country outside of his own?"

"He has not. But I myself have been educated in the States."

"Then it's your own resentment talking, maybe, and not the King's," Gabby dug. "Some frat party girl turn you down, Max?"

"No woman has ever turned me down," Max replied without ego.

"Well. That I do, believe," Gabby took a time out from the argument to admit. She instantly wished for the words back.

"Meaning?" he asked with a flirty grin glowing underneath that mug of his. Meant to... disarm her or... something. She certainly wasn't in the mood to argue anymore, so it was working.

"Meaning you're a tall drink of water, Max, everyone knows it. You got the whole quiet strength thing happening. Polite, poised," her mouth kept on and on. Maybe if she just said it, the thoughts would lose power, she distantly reasoned. "I'm sure you drenched the underwear of many a co-ed. And their teachers."

Max had a conflict of emotions going on in him at the moment. Shock, amusement, intrigue. A slight thread of disgust running through it all.

"Your servant is flattered by the Queen's compliment, but she must leave this vulgar tongue in America where it belongs if she is to become Queen."

Gabby rolled her eyes. Such a stick in the mud. A very regal hall monitor is what he was. And low-key rude. She was suddenly relieved she was marrying the other guy.

"Obviously, I was trying to make you uncomfortable, Max. No need to insult America over it."

"Why?"

"Because there's something fun about it."

Max huffed a laugh before he could stop himself. Gabby turned to him and smiled, her gaze pinned to his pearl white teeth. Not noticing how they were just sitting in the damn parking lot.

"I just hope that all the grace I'm expected to have for this situation will be returned to me, that's all," she said.

"I can assure you it will. Not only from the king but from the people of Manaf."

Gabby gave him a little grin of gratitude. She bumped his shoulder with hers as they sat.

"Promise you won't tell your boss I'm a slut for flirting with his vizier?" she teased.

Flirting? Was she flirting? His heart quickened and a swallow went down his throat involuntarily, as if he'd been overdue for it.

If the Queen was ever caught doing anything that could be remotely construed as flirting with another man, especially the king's vizier, she would be lucky to escape the palace with her life.

"My apologies if I misjudged you, my Queen," he somberly said.

Gabby sighed. "I apologize too. For speaking... too informally. In front of you," she added, just in case. "If I'd known just 24 hours ago that my days of frivolous words were quickly coming to an end..."

Max sympathized. "The Queen is always welcome to run her unfiltered thoughts by the king's vizier before she says them to anyone else."

Gabby laughed. "Thank you, Max. I'll hold you to that."

Aaaand they were still here. Once it seemed their conversation had come to a close, Max popped open his car door and surprisingly, Gabby remembered to stay put. He opened her car door and she took his outstretched hand.

The touch sent a single circuit of shock to her middle.

She forced herself to not look away from him, forced her energy to remain neutral as he warmly regarded her, looking apologetic.

"Tomorrow, my Queen. I beg you," his low voice crooned.

Tomorrow? What's a tomorrow? Oh, right. Tomorrow. The King.

"Very well, Mazigh," Gabby smiled as she sighed, her address getting more queen-like by the hour.

Mazigh's full name on her tongue hit his ears like a lullaby. He hastened around to the driver's side of her old beat-up Honda and opened the door.

"By the way, I don't know what the King of Ghassan said about us, but there are a lot of American women who would trade places with me in a heartbeat. Women with little to lose and little to look forward to."

"I take it you don't count yourself among these women."

"Not at all."

The Queen was beautiful, he noted, fighting the urge to run a finger down her jawline as she spoke. Young. Much younger than her twenty-five years.

"And what did you have to look forward to, young Asha, before we arrived?"

Max gazed at her profile as she looked away, a breeze blowing her hair about her ears.

"Freedom, Max. Freedom. Which means more to this girl than any palace."

Wordlessly she got in and started the surprisingly smooth engine without looking up. Max remained in the doorway.

"Until tomorrow, my Queen."

"Bright and early, Mazigh," the Queen replied with some backbone. "I mean it."

* * *

Max returned to his luxury room in Tampa's boutique 4-star hotel. He stripped off his dress shirt, his muscled physique a visual buffet gone to waste in the empty suite.

He found himself splashing water on his face and looking at himself in the mirror. He sighed.

He had exactly 48 hours to get an actual grip.

Leaving young Asha's presence was already making his bones feel heavier. Time slower.

But he stuffed down the trouble he was clearly in to focus on the task at hand.

It wasn't denial. It was life. And he'd suffered grim realities for most of it.

He would not be done in by an American-born Ashwari princess, her teetering maturity both turning him boneless and calling to his buried reckless youth.

He was, perhaps, too harsh with her. But it was getting harder to fool her. Harder to lie.

Everything he did and said around her was strange to him. He just wanted to be done with this part of the plan already.

He hopped into the spa-like tub and turned on the shower. Afterward, he picked up the hotel phone and rang the penthouse. The king picked up right away.

"My King."

"Where are we?"

"I acquired DNA samples from the mother and father. The Ashwari doctor has them now," Mazigh replied.

"What can he do for us?"

"Unfortunately without living parents to get samples from, it will be hard to determine her true parentage," Mazigh explained.

"But if the Princess's DNA does not match anyone else's, it will at least corroborate the story. I spoke to them at length and I am convinced from their testimony alone."

"Did you ask about her social circle?" the King asked.

"I did. The little sister was quite helpful."

"What did you find out?"

"She had many friends in high school, what the Americans call their secondary school. But because of her illegal status she was unable to apply to university, which is where most American girls learn to become promiscuous."

"A good sign."

"Indeed."

"No boyfriends?"

"The sister says that her parents did not permit dating for any of the children. Fairly standard for more conservative households. Once they turn 18, they often go to university or live on their own."

"But the Princess did neither."

"Correct. Her brother and sister attended school while Princess Asha worked. She entered the nursing program at a school for trades several years ago."

"We may have a problem, Mazigh."

"I already know."

"You do?" the King asked, surprised.

"The Queen and her sister have been researching you, your Majesty. On the internet."

Oh, that, he thought. "And?"

"And if they know the truth, they don't seem to be letting on."

"Fortunately, the world doesn't care much about Manaf beyond my father's gruesome death and my childhood ascendancy."

"Also, the passport won't be ready in 48 hours," Mazigh broke more news to him, piece by piece.

"Then we stick to the original plan," the King replied.

"Do you really want to force her to come with us?"

"I'm positive it won't come to that. Especially if the Princess comes to the king's hotel and speaks personally with him tomorrow."

Mazigh's eyes widened against his will, which the King could somehow see over the phone. Well, well. It seemed he was full of surprises.

"Will that be a problem?" King Khoury asked.

"...No. Actually. But yesterday you were adamant about maintaining a proper distance until we depart?" Mazigh tactfully reminded him. As if he could forget.

"Which we will continue to do. Do you object?"

The King's vizier chose his words carefully.

"Just counting the hours until we're back in the air, my liege." He wasn't alone.

"You're doing just fine," the King said. "But the Queen needs re-assurance if she is to leave her home for the unknown."

"Your Majesty—"

"The King will need his vizier there, of course. To fill in whatever information the King doesn't know."

Mazigh let out a deep sigh. He hadn't been in America for years. He wanted to eat a proper Cuban, not be forced to share the same space with the Queen, and continue to make a fool of himself.

But he knew there was no talking the King out of this, especially since it was his idea.

The sooner he could be done with this assignment, the better. But he kept his desires to himself.

"Of course, your Majesty. A brief meeting, I trust."

"Not *too* brief," the King advised. "At this point, the king's vizier has spent more time with the Queen than the king has. We don't want to give way to impropriety."

"Impropriety?" Mazigh raised an eyebrow.

"The appearance of it," the King clarified. Mazigh was dumbfounded.

"Speaking of which, the king is not to touch her. On this visit or any other," King Khoury added.

"...You're telling *me* this?"

"Just be ready tomorrow, Mazigh. The king will meet her here in his suite."

"Very well," he dutifully replied. The king hung up the phone without a word. Max looked at the receiver in disbelief. He shook his head.

"Speaking of impropriety," Max muttered, putting the phone down.

7

Chapter 7

The next day, Max arrived bright and early as instructed to the bright blue house on a quiet narrow street. He waited on the couch for Gabby to emerge from her room.

With advanced notice, the Ayenews had prepared an elaborate spread of traditional American and Ashwari breakfast items. Eggs, bacon, plenty of melon. Spicy shrimp. Rice patties.

"We were under the impression that the King would also be arriving," Gabby's mother began, obviously unimpressed with Max.

"Unfortunately, he was unable to accompany me. It will only be a brief visit."

"When do you expect you will be leaving?"

"Tomorrow," Max said, hoping not to sound too eager. "The King has never been this far away from his throne and he is anxious to return."

"Please allow us a final meal with our daughter," Gabby's mother held her chest, breathless as she referred to Gabby as "daughter." "She.... she's only known us as her home. I'm making a traditional Ashwari dinner. Enough to feed a King and his vizier, if they would like to join."

"We would be honored," Max smiled.

"Some of our friends would also like to come?"

"I do not think that's wise," he replied.

"Of course, sir."

"Perhaps once the King and Queen are officially married, and her political enemies are dealt with, she can return and visit with them openly."

"Perhaps back in our own country again," her mother dared to dream.

"The king of Manaf would very much look forward to that," Max said, examining closer the pictures on the wall in front of him. He got up from the dining room table to take a closer look.

He saw one of Gabby in a skimpy top and shorts, her legs impossibly long with a gleaming smile, standing outside on a platform as though it were the Olympics.

"Gabby was quite the track star in high school," her mother bragged.

The wall was littered with pictures of Gabby over the years. One wearing a cheerleading outfit as a little girl, still missing teeth. One as a pre-teen in a ruffly dress, wearing a sash. Always smiling. Achieving.

They were interrupted when Gabby emerged in a long flowing skirt and a halter top, her long straightened hair in a ponytail with long strands framing her face in the front.

Max's heart rose and fell at the sight of the young woman. Though he had only ever lived in the palace as a young man, he instinctively knew that he was experiencing the common man's courtship, sitting in the family room with the young Asha's parents, waiting for her to emerge.

73

Unfortunately, the first thing he noticed was that she was showing far too much for a Manafi queen. Her warm brown skin overwhelmed him. The notch between her cleavage taunted him.

If he didn't know better, he'd think she was trying to seduce the king, which offended him and would scandalize the king.

But just 36 hours in America was enough time to appreciate her modesty and poise. Their eyes locked and for a moment she seemed to look frightened.

"What?" she said.

"It's a bit... immodest," he plainly answered. "For an audience with the king."

The entire room stiffened.

"What do you suggest?" she asked without complaint.

"The skirt is fine, but the top will have to be changed."

"Long sleeves? Short?"

Max cleared his throat, feeling deeply awkward suddenly. Conversations like these were the attendants' job. *Just one more day.*

"The... cleavage is the issue. Not the sleeves."

Gabby looked down at herself with a scoff, as if to say "what cleavage?" She turned back to her room with her sister rushing behind in an unspoken offer of assistance.

Moments later, the pair returned. Gabby wore a wine-colored shirt that covered her up top but cut off at the midriff.

"What about this?" Gabby asked, as if ready to be denied.

"Fine," Max nodded, though he had to smile, relieved.

The Princess was testing the boundaries, most likely out of education rather than defiance.

But there was no need to worry. The midriff was permitted to be shown in Manaf and was commonly taken advantage of by the young women there. Max always found the reasoning a bit backward. If the goal was to preserve female modesty— and distractionless men by extension— then a bare midriff was no kind of solution.

But he imagined that women must've struck this compromise long ago. And that it pleased men to indulge a beautiful woman's desire to be admired. The color was beautiful against her and he made a mental note for the royal dressmaker.

"Great! Let's go," Gabby let out a breath. "*Ema*, I'll be back soon."

Her mother smiled at the affectionate address. Her true mother would be so proud, she thought. "Please tell the king how honored we were by his presence, and that we are more than happy to provide anything else he may need," she said as she followed them across the living room.

"Of course," Max nodded as the pair made their way out the door.

* * *

Gabby had only occasionally driven by the plush hotel that was a 20-minute drive across the turnpike surrounded by water, but she'd never been this close. She'd certainly never gone inside.

"I'm afraid there's another very important matter of etiquette that I've forgotten to tell you until now."

Gabby raised an eyebrow. "Which is?"

"The Princess may not speak until granted permission to do so. Or if the King addresses you first."

"I... okay."

"This extends to all. Including myself," Max was quick to expound.

"Then it's fortunate for all of us that I loathe small talk."

"I have noticed," he grinned, a lilt of approval in his voice.

Gabby giggled and shook her head, rolling her eyes. She wondered if these were just fancy royal red flags she was seeing. Was she really about to fly halfway around the world with these guys to a foreign, uncertain future? It seemed irresponsible. But secretly did little to deter her.

The lobby of the hotel had to be a hundred feet high in the middle. The surrounding balconies of each floor appeared endless.

The elevator powered them forcefully up to the top. When Gabby entered the penthouse suite, the king was already seated on the couch, well dressed in a black suit and skinny tie meant to convey casualness. They entered the living room and the king's long proud face shifted when Gabby entered his sight. He greeted the Princess with a warm white smile.

"Good afternoon, Princess Asha."

"Thank you for meeting with me again, your Majesty. I understand that's unusual," Gabby shyly smiled, testing out this newfound rule of theirs. When she gave Max a nervous glance he simply nodded his head with a warm grin of encouragement.

She assumed the rule simply meant she could not be the first one to begin an exchange, not that all her conversations would be interrogations. And she was right.

"It is I who should be thanking you, Princess. You light up the room with your beauty."

Max's grin waned.

"Same," she giggled sweetly, watching his reaction to her flirt. His tight mouth drew up in an adorable smirk. Max suppressed an eye-roll.

"You're practically Manafi already. You look beautiful."

"The Princess requested an audience with you yesterday," Max needlessly interjected.

"Indeed," the king nodded. "My vizier tells me that you've been doing research on me and my land."

"I have."

"Have you done any on your own land?" he asked, meaning Ashwari. Gabby understood.

"Some."

"So you do understand that Ashwari has been in the midst of a coup these twenty-three years?"

"Yes. My real father's general. General Olayinka. He's made it a religious conflict. The country is run by zealots."

"Only by proxy," the king corrected. "He pretends to be a revolutionary. But the same allies that ran your father run his General. Only the face of it has changed. General Olayinka is a dangerous man, who would kill you and anyone related to you if he knew you were alive," the king casually explained while making his tea, the tray of ingredients in front of him on the table.

"My apologies for arriving in such a... cryptic manner. Information of this magnitude has a way of traveling. We've done our best to be discreet, but we need to move quietly and quickly, for all our sakes."

"I understand. Thank you for indulging my concerns. My parents..." Gabby backtracked. "My... guardians... they kept a strict leash on us. We trusted no one who wasn't Ashwari friends or family. And now I'm being asked to do the opposite of all that, all while trusting that you are who you say you are. I'm afraid my naivete has made me doubly paranoid."

"Were you unable to verify my identity from your research?" the king asked in a commanding tone.

"Well, unfortunately, you're no longer an adorable child wearing a giant king robe, so Wikipedia is useless to me right now."

The King and his vizier exchanged a look and the two men seemed to relax. The King sat back in his chair.

"What would you like to know, Princess?"

"Anything, of course. About you. I realize we're pressed for time, but... I'd like to know what I'm in for. As far as being a queen. Being your wife."

The king sat up, as if in fear that he'd been too informal up to now. "As a queen, you will be required to accompany me to public appearances. Of course, Manafi culture is much different from America, as you can probably imagine," he explained with kind eyes turning bright brown in the glare of the sun. "You will be representing the King in every way, and so you will have to be much more conscious of your manner of dress and speech. Outfits like the one you're wearing now, for example, will be a thing of the past."

Max inwardly cringed as Gabby looked down at herself. After his lecture from earlier, she was likely thinking the worst.

"The king, I believe, is referring to the casual dress style, rather than your modesty, Princess."

"Yes, forgive me," the king seemed to stutter. "You will be dressed in only the finest fabrics."

"You're saying my clothes are shabby, my King?"

In his mind, Max smacked his own forehead.

"They are... adequate. For a young American girl, but not for a queen."

"I'm only teasing, your Majesty."

"Ah," he smiled. "My vizier tells me your sense of humor will take some getting used to."

"Does he, now?" Gabby raised her eyebrows in surprise as she turned to look at Max, who maintained a stoic air as he ignored her gaze.

Gabby felt the urge to taunt him further but she relented, turning back towards the king. "You keep referring to me as young, but we are only a few years apart, your Majesty."

"True. But your family tells me that because of your true identity, they sheltered you much more than they did the other children."

Gabby kept her face and voice neutral. "Did they?"

The king furrowed his brow, worried he had offended her. "Yes. Has this not been your experience?"

Gabby shrugged ever so slightly. "Faraj was a boy, so naturally he enjoyed more freedom. Kenzie was younger than me. For a while I assumed they simply had become more lax once she came along," Gabby recalled as she fiddled with a thread on her skirt. "Some of it was self-imposed. I guess I internalized much of the fear of the outside world they imposed on me. But I changed all that once I graduated high school and they told me the truth— well, the half-truth— that I wasn't really theirs. Since then I've tried to become as independent as possible."

"Of course."

"I realize that compared to being king for over half of your life, it must seem childish by comparison."

"Does my referring to you as young offend you?"

"Not really, I just find it curious, your Majesty," Gabby politely replied.

"You are right. Being a king for so long makes everyone around me seem young by comparison, but especially you," the king mused. "For being an older bride, you seem quite young."

Max squirmed in his chair and cleared his throat.

"An older bride, huh?" Gabby smiled cordially. "Yes, I imagine girls are married off quite young on your side of the world."

"Traditionally, yes. Not as much anymore. Manaf has adopted more modern ideals of the West in that sense. But I've always said a king should marry young."

Max rubbed his forehead with closed eyes.

"I see."

"To better ensure plenty of heirs are born to him. Nothing inappropriate, of course. Your sister, for example, is a prime age."

Oh my God.

"...My sister," Gabby repeated, intrigued by the king's logic.

"Indeed."

Max was practically having an out of body experience. Worse, he was too speechless to get the conversation back on track in a way that wouldn't get him reprimanded. Miraculously, Gabby remained focused.

"So this will be a... will we... consummate our relationship?"

Max felt such shame as a shiver shot through him at her question that he had to look down at the coffee table that separated them.

She asked in a way that let Max know she'd been dying to ask it since they got there. The king picked up on his vizier's mood as he chose his next words carefully.

"Naturally, if we are to produce legitimate heirs," he said matter-of-factly.

"That is, if I'm not too long in the tooth, your Majesty," Gabby teased with a monotone voice.

"I've offended you," the king smiled with a tilted head. Max couldn't smile if he wanted to. Now she was teasing the king instead of him.

"Not at all. Just... a little more insecure about my position than when we first met."

"I'm not explaining myself well, I'm afraid. Max must be slacking in his duties to properly inform the Princess," the King implied with a look to his vizier.

"I wanted to hear it from the King's mouth," Gabby came to Max's rescue.

"Still, you must forgive Max," the king insisted. "He's more than capable of being my representative when I'm not here. It is his *whole* job, in fact."

Max's jaw clenched and the King relinquished a smile as if enjoying the taunt.

"I've never put Max in such an extraordinary situation. Such repeated exposure to a beautiful young woman has short-circuited his brain," the King flirted as he continued to give Max a hard time.

Max's calm sea of an expression worked against him this time, betraying guilt rather than indifference. Gabby tried to stifle her smile, even as his reaction released a flurry of butterflies inside.

She quickly switched her gaze back to the king who was already looking at her, as if caught. She wasn't sure how to feel about that.

When the king gave her a wink and a smirk she was even more confused. Her body trembled and shocked, as if sending every alarm bell it could in total helplessness.

"Allow me to make it clear," he continued assertively. Your job will be to represent the King publicly and raise the King's royal offspring. Apart from that, you'll have little to do. You will, of course, have servants, attendants, nurses, midwives, and anything your heart desires."

"Ashwari," Gabby said.

The king's expression wilted a bit."What about it?"

"What will you do about it?"

The king raised his eyebrows diplomatically, as if indignant at her questioning him. "I will make negotiations of surrender with the General that he will likely agree to. And hopefully, bring him to justice with the help of the people."

"Hopefully?"

"Indeed. Once we return to Manaf, I will announce that I have chosen a queen and that we are to be married. Within the week. Once we are successfully wed, we will announce your identity to anyone who will listen."

"There's only one problem with all of that."

"Which is?"

"How am I going to get on a plane without a passport?"

The two men looked at each other again. The king appeared to remember himself.

"Well, Mazigh?" he asked with masked irritation.

"We've spoken to the embassy. We're in the process of handling it," Max gently re-assured.

Gabby stopped, her shoulders straightened.

"So I'll be free to go by... tomorrow? Seems so unreal."

"The embassy understands our need for discretion. And haste."

"I had no idea America-Manaf relations were so good," she commented.

"Neither did we!" the king smiled uncharacteristically. Gabby found herself giggling.

At some moments the king seemed dark and severe and imposing. And other times he seemed like a kid without a care in the world.

She told herself it was the effect of Max on him, who seemed incapable of being rattled. Or tickled. By anything. There was something naturally amusing about the pair of them.

"Do you have any other questions, Princess?" Max quietly urged her from the corner. It made her feel self-conscious, as though she'd wasted the King's time.

"Yes," she soldiered on. "Does the King want to marry me?"

While Max wished to be invisible, the king answered emphatically with a nod.

"Yes. Very much."

"I hope I can make you happy, my King," Gabby replied.

Max's heart exploded and ran down his insides in a pool of mush.

"By the King's throne, that's one thing you will never have to worry about, my Queen," the king smiled warmly.

"Will you be joining us for my farewell dinner tonight, your Majesty?"

"Mazigh?" the king inquired.

"If the king can behave himself," Max muttered.

"*Nonsense*," he exclaimed in Arabic, "I'm doing very well, aren't I, Princess Asha?" he asked, his eyes beaming, with a mischievous grin.

"You're doing very well, your Majesty," Gabby laughed. "You've been here two days and you're practically an American," she flattered him. He gestured to her with an outstretched arm as he taunted Max with a look of "I told you so." Max remained unamused.

Gabby continued to giggle. It was the first real revelation of the king's personality and she was intrigued. Charmed. She wasn't getting the hot flashes, but even with his regal and studious manner, she got the impression the king would do his best to make everything fun. A flurry of excitement about the future rushed through her.

"I will return the Princess to her parent's house, then. I will be back to retrieve you for the dinner."

"Very well, Mazigh," he nodded. "Farewell, Princess Asha. Until tonight," he offered without getting up.

Gabby stood, unconsciously smoothing out her skirt. "Until tonight, your Majesty."

Max stood to escort her out and Gabby stood with him. The king watched from his chair as the two made their way out of the penthouse living room.

"Max. I need a word with you. Alone," the king added. Gabby turned to Max with a shy turn of her head.

"I can meet you downstairs. In the lobby."

"No. Wait for me in the hall," Max instructed her, closing the door softly behind him.

* * *

Back in the living area, the king was still on the couch, having picked up the phone to order room service. He'd retrieved a handful of grapes from the end table behind him. Max slowly sauntered over to the king until he was standing directly in front of him. The king leaned away from Max's imposing stance, chewing.

"*Madha*?"

"Are you enjoying yourself, your majesty?"

"Very much," the king chewed.

"America has turned you into quite the court jester."

"This *'amahq* plan of yours has," the king corrected, snapping the remaining cluster of grapes off. "I've decided to enjoy myself," he said, popping another grape in his mouth.

"I have always wanted to go to Florida. Does it not remind you of home?"

"No," Max replied.

"I'm surprised there are still palm trees this far north."

"Did her lab results come back yet?" Max asked.

"You mean... her exam?"

"Yes."

"I thought his Majesty didn't want to know?"

"Tell me," Max demanded.

"The hymen wasn't broken."

Max's jaw clenched. Everything in him wanted to simply gather the Princess up in a potato sack and hurry her to Bel's private plane. He'd been haunted by her big dark eyes since he first laid eyes on her in that silly shower cap and wrapped in only a towel.

He didn't like America, if Florida was any indication. It was sticky along with its heat. The women walked around naked and the men permitted it, feasting their eyes and weakening their own resolves. He wanted the Princess out of this environment as soon as possible.

He was glad he wasn't the king right now. Because if it were in his power he would have her delivered to the King's chamber with nothing on but a wedding sash, naked and confused. And angry, as she most assuredly would be. He'd yet to see evidence of that Otieno blood, hot and proud, but he knew it was there. He tried and failed not to picture it.

Max stared as the king continued to chew contentedly, until he had to furrow his brow again.

"What now?"

Max did a quick shoulder shrug and shook his head. "What

were you thinking?"

"What do you mean?"

"Did you really mention the sister??"

The king raised his arms in a shrug of defense. "What are you upset about? Everything went fine."

Max continued to loom over him. "You will stop flirting with the Princess at once."

"Oh, honestly," the king rolled his eyes. "If anything she was flirting with *me.*"

"Keep your voice down," Max said, his flared nostrils the only sign of annoyance. "She thinks you're the King. Of course, she wants to create a rapport with you."

"Should I not indulge her?"

"You're supposed to *pretend* to be me," Max said.

"*Yes, I know how this works, I invented it, remember?*" the king returned in hushed tones of Arabic. "If I *pretend* to be you any longer, she will fear she has just agreed to marry a closeted homosexual, and never get on a plane with us tomorrow."

Max knit his brow with a far-off look. "About that..."

The king raised his eyebrow as he chewed.

Max took a paranoid glance at the hotel room door. "...I need you to pretend to be the King a little longer."

The king remained motionless. "How long?"

"Tonight, of course. And then once we take off tomorrow."

The king shook his head after a long while, waiting for the rest of this stellar plan.

"Until... when?"

"I don't know," Max admitted.

The king rolled his head to one side, his eyes wide. "I can't very well fool the people of Manaf, my King. Unless you plan to end this charade in mid-air—"

"If she handles it well, we will tell her the truth. If not... I don't want her hating me just yet."

The king shook his head in dismay with a deep breath at the thought of this getting even more absurd than it already was. "Emir—"

"She will be mad at you, until further notice."

"So you mean to make me the bearer of bad news until we get home?"

"Correct."

The king gave him a frustrated chuckle.

"You can handle it, Mazigh. You have been through two wars."

"So have you, your Majesty," the king replied. "Am I to suffer your eye-daggers indefinitely?"

"What eye daggers?"

The king scoffed and got up from his place on the sofa.

"You have nothing to worry about, you know," the king said in response to Max's unspoken concern. Instead of being embarrassed, Max leaned into his insecurities.

"She seemed rather eager to laugh at your levities."

"As she should. I am quite humorous, unlike you," he teased. "I like her, your Majesty."

"I am so glad."

"She's only *trying* to fall in love with me. She's trying *not* to fall in love with you."

"Enough, Mazigh," said Max.

"It's true, my King. You risk ruining your relationship before it begins. I would not endeavor to deceive her much longer, if I were you."

Max made his way back to the hotel room door. "Then thank goodness you are not me."

8

Chapter 8

Waiting outside the penthouse suite, Gabby's denial was quickly turning into an unbearable itch she wanted to scratch. Being in the same room with both of them again for only the second time, she was starting to worry.

She could've sworn the King was much more powerful and dashing the first time they met.

It'd only been a few days. How could that have worn off so quickly?

She's spent too much time with Max alone, she deduced. She'd gotten to know one and not the other.

That will all change once they leave. In fact, this might be the last time she'll ever see Max so much. She gave her gold pennant necklace of a crescent moon a twirl as she paced.

She'll have her whole life to get to know the King, and build the same fondness, she resolved. Suddenly, Gabby turned to see Max coming through the penthouse door when she heard it open.

"Were you in trouble back there?" Gabby teased.

"Why would I be in trouble?"

"I don't know. You were in there a while."

Max grinned. "He wanted to discuss our departure tomorrow."

"Ah."

"You don't seem enthusiastic," he said, gesturing towards the elevator.

Gabby shrugged, slowly walking. "Just doesn't seem real, is all. Seems a bit... wrong."

"Wrong?"

"I don't know. Off. Irresponsible. My supervisor thinks I'll be there tomorrow."

"You have more pressing matters," he replied inflexibly. The elevator doors closed and the car was quiet as it quickly plummeted them toward the lobby.

"I know. It's just that I made commitments."

"I understand. But you made them unknowingly. You couldn't anticipate this."

"Couldn't I?" Gabby argued, watching the numbers as they changed. she could see Max in her peripheral, watching her. He never took his eyes off her, it seemed. She thought perhaps it was cultural. The King seemed to do the same. But it was unnerving in such a small space.

"It was my idea to go to school, to undertake more obligations. My parents were right all along."

"You were both right."

"I just wish I could tell the school. So they could understand."

"They will soon enough," he said as the elevator doors opened. "Soon enough the world will know."

They walked out of the lobby, back towards the car. "Think we could stop and get something to eat?" she asked.

89

"Of course. Forgive my thoughtlessness."

"No, it's okay. There's one place I want to go before I leave, and it's not far from here. So it works out."

Max put Datz into the car's GPS.

"Do they have crab in Manaf?" Gabby wondered, already preparing herself for new cuisine.

"Of course," said Max.

"Where did you go to school again?" she asked inquisitively.

The King recalled his vizier's history. "Duke University," he formerly announced.

"North Carolina, huh? That must've been... interesting, you going to school in the South," Gabby grinned.

"It was," Max lied.

"Duke was on my shortlist. Before that whole 'you're undocumented' conversation."

When they arrived at their destination, Gabby ordered for both of them. Deviled crab for her and a smoked mullet sandwich for him.

"Did the King meet your expectations this morning?" Max suddenly changed the subject as the food arrived.

"He did," Gabby smiled.

"And?"

"And... he seems like a good guy."

Max gave her a smirk, which caused Gabby's permanently plastered smile.

"What?" she asked.

"Nothing," he shook his head. He bit into his sandwich.

"C'mon, Max. Give me your unfiltered thoughts."

"No," he sternly answered as he chewed. Gabby's cheeks were hurting from the smiles.

"Your Queen demands it," she said.

Max wiped his mouth with a slow, regal air. *Didn't know eating sandwiches could be sexy, but okay,* Gabby thought.

"Do you really wish to make the king happy?" he wondered.

Gabby furrowed her brow. Of all the things she expected him to say, it wasn't that.

"Of course. Why, did I seem too... thirsty?" she asked.

"Thirsty?"

"You know. Desperate."

Max grinned fondly. "No, Princess. You were perfect."

"Really?"

"Right out of a storybook."

Gabby's cheeks grew hot. She wanted to make light of his comment but found she was too preoccupied with the immediate analysis of it. She could think of no convincing way to shrug it off, so in the end, she just... didn't. Instead, she slurped the last of her soda and gave her mouth something to do. Likewise, Max fiddled with his coleslaw, fork in hand.

"In the future, I think it's best for you to be direct with the King. Try not to resort to flattery."

"Flattery?"

"The King is aware that the two of you just met. And you are a woman of stature, a princess. No need to cater to his ego to win his affection with flattering words. He has already chosen you."

"I appreciate the advice, Max, but I meant what I said."

Max fiddled with his coleslaw some more, feigning objectivity. "You went from insulting his honor to wishing to please him in two days."

"I know. But I want to show him that I can play ball."

"...Because he provided you with the documents you asked for," he filled in.

Gabby flexed her shoulders. "So? You showed up at my door

saying fantastical things, Max. I was trying to be sensible," Gabby defended, getting used to Max's confrontational way of conversing. "There's no time or place for courtship, as you're so fond of reminding me. How else did you expect the King to earn my trust overnight?"

The sick feeling returned when she mentioned trust.

"You're right, Princess. Forgive me."

"You're quite protective of the King, Mazigh," Gabby smiled.

"Perhaps."

"Perhaps? The only time you're willing to rip my head off is on his behalf."

"Touché, Princess."

"I find it quite interesting that of all people to be worried about running game, it's you rather than me."

"The King has had his fair share of game runners," Max stretched the turn of phrase to its peak. "He can smell it a mile away."

"Then it has made him overly paranoid," Gabby insisted. "The King and I are going to be married." A random couple turned their heads and looked in their direction overhearing her words. She noticed but ignored them.

"It's not flattery to want to start this relationship the best way possible. Obviously, I don't know him, but I'm going to. I want to do well at this. Besides, I'm not blind," she added.

Max raised an eyebrow at her words. "You find the king attractive."

"Of course," Gabby answered, suddenly feeling self-conscious at her admission.

"Has the king moistened your underwear also?" he suddenly asked, munching on coleslaw, his smolder on display.

Gabby froze, trying to stave off oh so many emotions. Shock, shame, fear of the incredible arousal coming over her in an abrupt wave, mostly manifesting itself as sweaty palms and panic.

She heard Max's low chuckle from some disembodied place outside of herself. He retrieved a napkin and wiped his fingers, his stoic expression relaxed.

"The Princess dishes out what she herself cannot take."

Gabby wielded an adorable smile to shield her embarrassment. It certainly wouldn't be appropriate to tease him back. But why was he asking for it?

"Fine. I've learned my lesson," Gabby fiddled with her food. "But since you asked... it takes a lot more than that to drench my underwear," Gabby scoffed with a sip of her drink.

Max let out a hearty laugh. I *can't wait to find out*, was what he nearly said.

He was having far too much fun not being the King. This was his and Mazigh's childhood games on steroids. To go longer than a day being someone else was simply unheard of.

But here he was, out in public with a woman with no connec-tions, sans chaperones. And no one in the slightest cared. As if the entire population was in on the prank.

"If kings do not arouse you then your male acquaintances have my sympathies," Max grinned.

"They deserve them, I hate to say."

Max laughed again. "If the Princess has taken no suitors, it must be because you have refused them."

"I've gotten a few brave offers."

"Only a few?"

"If this is your way of saying you find me attractive, then thank you, Max."

He ignored her polite words. "I imagine your manner intimidates them further."

"My manner?"

"You have your father's fierce nature. The king's vizier has experienced it first hand."

Gabby grinned sheepishly. "I'm not like this with everyone. Hardly anyone."

"And how shall I advise the King to win your affections?" he asked with a sleepy gaze.

"Nice try."

"I am sincerely curious, Princess. If you are not impressed with riches or status, youth, or beauty, then what captivates you?"

Gabby could barely look in Max's direction, shrinking under the light of his sincere question, so direct that it seemed more demanding than wondering. But patient all the same. *Do whatever it is that you're doing right now,* she thought.

"If I knew the answer to that, you and I probably wouldn't be sitting here." She nodded in his direction. "What do you know about my father's fierce nature?"

"The people of Manaf remember King Otieno well and remember him being unseated. I was a young boy of seven when it happened."

"Did his palace have green windows?" she suddenly asked.

Max searched his own memories. He'd also visited once, invited by the General as a teen. He'd been King nearly ten years at the time.

"I do not think so, Princess."

"I have this... early memory. Of green windows. Going up a green wall like a chain pattern."

"You think this is a memory of you in the Ashwari palace?"

"Don't know. But I thought I'd try. I have a lot of disjointed memories, which is apparently not normal," she continued, fiddling with her straw. "Voices of many people other than my parents. Almost as though I didn't have parents. Or as though an entire village were my parents. And then suddenly... it's as though I did. And it's all sunshine and beaches and a brother. And then a sister. Like all that was some infant hallucination. I still dream about it quite a lot," she said, discreetly wiping a tear.

Max inched his way around the outdoor table bench until he was next to her.

"King Khoury was also waited on by many maids and nurses throughout his childhood when he was the Prince. He was rarely let outside the palace walls. I imagine if that was all taken away early enough, and replaced with something entirely different, that part of his life would also be without context."

She wanted to kiss him right then and there. He was so close and he smelled divine. He cared about her. He understood her.

The moment emblazoned itself in her mind and she knew that a crush was forming. It wasn't her first, but it'd been a while. And as usual, it was terribly misdirected.

Naturally, she wished the king could make her feel the same way. Yet on some level, she liked that her head wasn't in the clouds when it came to dealing with him. She certainly had no indication that she was much more than an asset to him.

"Do you know why they call it coleslaw?" Max suddenly asked.

"No, why?" Gabby replied.

"I was asking you."

"Oh," Gabby snickered. "I don't know."

Max relinquished his seat next to hers. "We should head back, Princess" he replied.

Gabby took a deep breath and smiled. "Of course."

* * *

"*Ema*, how come you never talked about my mother to me?"

Max dropped her back home, where her family had already started preparations for dinner that night. He immediately left to retrieve the king for the family's farewell dinner. Gabby helped her surrogate mother cut vegetables in the kitchen, usually a silent task.

"Not even anonymously. As a friend of yours."

As soon as she asked, looking into her mother's distressed expression, she knew the answer. Still, she smiled.

"Would you like me to now?"

Gabby nodded.

"Your mother was to me what Mackenzie is to you now. A sister, five years younger than I. Her family moved from Ethiopia into our small village and our mothers formed a bond. My mother was also Ethiopian. She became like one of us," she said, adding strips of ginger to a boiling pot as Gabby sliced radishes.

"We grew up together. She was an only child. A great beauty. We called her *dnake*. She was the baby. Her father, your grandfather sheltered her, much like I did you. He was a doctor."

"Why did you leave Ashwari?" Gabby wondered.

She smiled. "Your mother was the one who convinced me. She loved America. When I had the opportunity to go to school here I jumped at it. Your mother wanted to move to Florida with me after she graduated."

"What happened?" Gabby prodded.

"King Otieno happened," she replied ominously.

"How did they meet?"

"They met each other at university. She said the first time she laid eyes on him he fell off the fence he was sitting on."

"Awww," Gabby smiled. "So they were in love?"

"I assume so. She certainly was. But things changed once they married."

"How so?" asked Gabby.

"When they married, he was only the prince. The rise to power changed their relationship, or maybe just changed the man. He became jealous. Controlling. Abusive."

"Leon, they're here," Gabby's father bellowed. Leon was her surrogate father's nickname for her mother.

"They're early," Gabby said, her stomach rising and falling. It was starting to become a habit whenever they came around.

"Faraj, keep them company."

"Let Dad do it, *Ema*," Faraj whined.

"Don't be lazy!"

"Mom, you know Raj is only here to eat," Gabby shook her head. Faraj mushed her head on the way to the door.

"Make sure Kenzie's wearing something presentable."

"She's not the one marrying him, Mom," Gabby scoffed.

"The other one must be available," her mother lowly schemed. Gabby's stomach jolted.

Max?

"She's... not his type," Gabby insisted.

"Sure he is, he is rich."

"I guess," Gabby mused. "But he's stern and disciplined and Mackenzie is... too young. And silly."

"Who's silly?" Mackenzie suddenly materialized in the kitchen.

"No one," Gabby muttered. Her mother watched curiously as she walked into the living room to greet their guests.

"Did you know they used Bel Hafiz's plane? That means you're gonna get to meet the CEO of MeTV. Like tomorrow, probably," Faraj said to her as she sat demurely across from the King and Max at the table. Again, the two of them in her house looked like elves visiting hobbits.

"Hello again... Max," Gabby was careful not to address the king first.

"Princess," Max grinned.

"Very good," commented the king.

"Thank you, Your Majesty, I try. And hello," Gabby said, turning to answer her brother. "Faraj, he's not the CEO anymore, Grayson Davis is—"

"Okay, the founder then."

"and I'm pretty sure you have to use his proper title now."

"...Not in America."

Gabby froze for a moment and then waved her hand in surrender. "Okay, well, say it wrong then."

"I will," Faraj quickly retorted. Their vaudeville bicker routine garnered a laugh from the two men.

As food began arriving, so did more house guests. Soon the table was full. Her mother had no place to sit, but was still in the kitchen heating dishes.

"So tomorrow is the big day," Faraj babbled. He was taking Father's place as the competent conversationalist in the house. "Gabby, you ready?"

"No. But I'm ready to do something... life-changing. Past ready, actually."

"Well, we're gonna miss you, little sis."

"Sure, you are," Gabby rolled her eyes as he grabbed her by the shoulders.

"She's gonna be back," Mackenzie scoffed. "And I'm damn sure coming to visit."

"No doubt."

Their mother had been busy hustling food from the kitchen to the table until finally, she borrowed a stool from the kitchen island. The king arose to offer his chair but she demanded he remain seated. She took a seat in front of her tepid plate as Faraj politely threw the conversation back to their guests.

"So, this was your first time in America, your Majesty?"

"Indeed," the king replied.

"How are you enjoying it?"

"Very much."

"He's being polite," Gabby chewed. Her siblings laughed.

"You are going to love Manaf, *mare*. It's like a paradise."

"You've been, *Baba*?" Mackenzie addressed their father.

"Many times, before I joined the army. The King of Manaf had just married your mother, may she rest."

"May she rest," the men nodded.

"Everyone wanted to go to Manaf back then."

"Ashwari became a place for Manafi to find brides, as I recall," Max spoke up.

"It did, for a little while," Gabby's father nodded, smiling. She watched and waited for the memory to turn bitter as it always did, without fail.

"Otieno put a stop to that," he cryptically added with a sip of black coffee.

Bingo. The chatter at the table died. Gabby felt an odd sense of responsibility knowing now that they were speaking of her real father.

"We should review the plan for tomorrow morning, Princess. In case we run into some... unforeseen challenges," the king began in a calm manner. Gabby felt a tension in Max's gaze across from her. She eyed one then the other.

"Is the passport not ready yet, my King?" Gabby asked.

She heard the clinking of silverware all around the table. She looked up and saw her parents perfectly still, their version of having their jaws on the floor. Mackenzie and Faraj looked at each other.

She realized no one had been privy to her royal etiquette coaching. Or her first meeting with the King. Nor had she brought it up at home. She must've sounded like a different person to them.

The King hadn't noticed at all. He looked over at Max, as if reminding him it was his job to answer pedestrian questions.

"Unfortunately it's taking more time than we were told," Max said.

"So what do we do?" Gabby asked.

"Not to worry. We're taking a private plane. We will inform the customs agent once we're on board that your passport is in process. Our pilot will contact international airspace once we take off."

"International airspace?" Gabby skeptically repeated.

"Yes, my Queen."

"I don't think you should leave so soon without a passport, *mare*. Things go wrong."

"He's a King, Mother," Gabby sheepishly argued. She didn't think it was all that responsible either, but leave it to Mother to force Gabby to defend strangers.

"The last thing you need to do is give U.S. Immigration a reason to lock you up. Or worse, send you back to Ashwari with nothing."

"I won't let that happen," the king replied with a reassuring smile.

"With all due respect, your Majesty, I've kept Asha safe all these years. One foolish move could undo all of that," her mother bravely countered. Gabby's safety was the one subject that could put her on edge.

"Leonida... Gabby will be the King's responsibility now. I'm sure he wants no harm to come to the girl," Gabby's father spoke up in a rare public display of assertiveness.

No one dared look up. They ate in silence, suddenly reminded why they didn't often entertain outsiders. Gabby's mother was silent for a moment, then quietly excused herself from the table. Gabby and her siblings sat awkwardly at the table.

"Please excuse my wife, your Majesty," Gabby's father began, "She hasn't yet prepared herself for the day that protecting the Queen's only daughter is finally over."

The king nodded in understanding. "Your wife has my sympathies."

* * *

Gabby finally laid in bed, blowing the breath out of her cheeks.

The King and his vizier were gone, the dishes were clean, her chores were done, and everyone was sleeping. Or so she hoped. At least she was finally alone.

She hated sharing a wall with her sister on one side and her brother on the other. She hated when every single family member was home when the urge hit. This was going to be the last night in this house for heaven knew how long, and she'd never been so glad.

She tossed and turned, getting ready to give in and do what she was obviously about to. Because she was so wired that she wasn't sure she would ever go to sleep again. And the rain outside her window was steady and ethereal. And she couldn't stop reliving the afternoon she spent with the king and his vizier. She'd endured the dull ache rolling around in her loins all day, practically from the moment she woke up. Or had it started from the day before?

She wanted more. That much she knew. But of what? It was all fun and games, all larping when they arrived. Now it was real. Now she had to be focused. And that meant no more flirting with the vizier.

No more "innocent" comments about moist underwear, which she'd now had all day. No more fishing for his compliments or making him laugh or say something outrageous. No more enabling his pity or comfort.

He was unwaveringly loyal to the king. She was practically a child to him. A vulgar child. She didn't even know if he approved of the marriage. And it was likely he would never show his true feelings about it.

Slowly her hand ventured below her blanket and hovered around her mound, feeling her thighs.

Picturing the king was far too weird. She didn't know him. She respected him. She didn't know how their relationship could possibly turn sexual, but she didn't doubt he was capable. She liked that. Maybe in time, he could give her butterflies. Seeing his smooth sable skin all over for the first time. His hard dick. Desire in his eyes, rather than patronizing diplomacy.

Picturing Max was... not allowed.

Why the fuck would he bring up her moist underwear?

Then he chuckled. He knew what he'd done. He didn't respect her. She was a vulgar American.

Or maybe... her comment had been on his mind. Longer than it should have been.

No, it was much more likely he'd given her a taste of her own

102

medicine. And she didn't like it.

What captivates you? he'd asked. On the king's behalf. Almost as if the king did nothing on his own behalf. Because he had Mazigh to do it all for him. Probably not the thing she was trying not to picture right now, though.

She wasn't even sure she wanted to picture Max in a sexual way, were it even possible. She wouldn't even know the first thing to anticipate. Max probably liked young Manafi women who were light-skinned and smiley and willing. Experienced. He didn't have the same restrictions a king had. Didn't have a kingdom to worry about. He could marry who he wanted. Or never marry.

He was definitely packing, though.

Yikes. Just the idea of it sent shocks to her middle. Max was a big dude. Big and tall. She relived seeing him standing in the nursing home lobby, tall and fit and commanding. With a better waistline than her. Maybe all Manaf men were like that. Maybe they all had big dicks. Another thing for her to worry about. Max would be patient with her, though. Or, you know, whoever.

He was a fucking thing of beauty. She didn't want to picture him naked, but if he shows up tomorrow in another dress shirt, she might fucking die. These weren't boys, these were fucking men. *Stop saying fuck.*

The king thought she was beautiful but old. He would be patient for a while, but that would probably wane in time. Everything about him seemed like a facade to get her to go with them.

She took a breath and tried to close her eyes and focus. Why was she being so weird in her own brain, like they were somewhere watching her? Judging her? If Max were here right now he probably wouldn't even be phased. He'd probably dutifully turn around in his chair until she was done. But would he be listening?

Fuck, she whispered. This was destined to be the weirdest self-pleasuring session ever. Forget the fantasies, she just needed to release this weird tension. She tried thinking of anything else as she rubbed. Anyone. But it was no use. The more she needed to come, the more dependent she became on images of Max, the sound of his voice, saying whatever she could invent from memory. Just now he was urging her to come. Calling her princess. He wasn't turned on. He just wanted to help. Wanted her release.

She was wetter than she'd ever been in her life. Her movement became wild. She jerked her hips upward, wiggling and slapping her clit like some trained animal. It felt so fucking good. She realized she'd forgotten to lock the door but it wasn't enough to stop her. Tonight would probably be the night for someone to barge in. But she was getting on a plane tomorrow, so fuck it.

"I'm gonna come for you," she began to whisper, again and again. In her mind, he begged her to let him see. He was desperate for it. Desperate as she was.

Her body seized upward, her neck craned back and her back bent until her head was upside down like she was being exorcised. Maybe she was. She had to be.

This had to be the last time she did that. She'd never come so hard and so long, with her imagination restricted to just a disembodied voice. It filled her with a sense of dread.

Whatever she thought she could ignore about Max clearly wasn't working because it didn't matter. He was trouble. And once she was queen, she was even more trouble. Kenzie was right, she could probably get them both killed. If he wanted to help her now, the best thing he could do was stay away.

He'd assured her things would be different once they got to Manaf. One plane ride and she could focus on Ashwari. She wouldn't see the king until the wedding. And hopefully, she would never have to look at Max again.

9

Chapter 9

T he next morning Gabby's father woke her up before anyone in the house was awake. He made her his signature waffles and sat in the sunroom saying nothing when she sauntered out of her room early, enjoying the quiet of the rest of the house while everyone slept. She'd slept little and got up at her body's clock. She and her father were always the early risers.

Her plate of waffles were perched atop the stove. From the kitchen island, she spotted him on the porch and reluctantly made her way outside, trying not to focus on the finality of it all. Cicadas chirped like a movie score in the distance as her father looked up at her with a smile. Gabby was quiet with dread as she sat, hoping this day wouldn't be the emotional drain it was already shaping up to be.

"You were my first little girl," he suddenly began.

Well, so much for that. Gabby turned away as she dabbed her tears, the sounds of early morning birds right outside the screened-in porch.

"From the time you came into our lives, you were searching

for what your purpose might be. Is it dance, is it cheerleading, is it track, is it being president? And every time you quit, you would be the saddest girl. More sad than anyone. I knew it was because you had to cross it off your list. It wasn't who you were. The older you got without any clues to this grand plan you felt a part of, the more I had to watch you get discouraged. Each year was like a trail growing cold. And I want to say I'm sorry for not telling you. We couldn't have you going off, telling your friends you were a Princess. Even if they didn't believe you. It really was a matter of life and death."

Gabby's father sniffed away his emotion as he continued.

"Your mother feels guilty for smothering you. She knows she has undermined you at times. She was so focused on keeping her promise to your mother. It's easy to hide a baby. But the older you got, the harder it became for her to let you take the reins of your own life. You, still at home at 25, with no prospects, no way to support yourself, it's not what I wanted for you. But it seemed to work out, didn't it *mare*? Your mother wins again."

Gabby laughed through her emotion, still too raw to add touching sentiments of her own. For some reason, it felt silly to thank them. They were obviously obliged to do it and besides, "thank you" wasn't enough. It felt burdensome but motivating. She had to do more than just be thankful. She had to thrive.

"Now you will be a queen. As you always were. I wish you were better prepared for it, Gabby. I do. The King, I trust, will take you the rest of the way."

The King. Anxiety filled her lungs like water. She could do this. She tested herself with an image of her deciding to stay. Going in to work-study as though nothing happened.

She recoiled. The decision was made.

"You don't have to say goodbye, *Abba*," her voice wavered.

"I'll be back, you know I will."

"I know. But I will say goodbye anyway. I'm happy to say it."

* * *

That morning at the airport, King Khoury was straddling the relief of boarding King Bel's private plane with Gabby in tow, and the anxiety of not yet being in the air. The turbines wailed as they made their way across the tarmac.

The wind blew Gabby's hair all around as the airline crew carried the few bags of belongings that she brought with her. She wasn't attached to many things. Just the things that carried memories and reminded her of home. She put her sister in charge of making sure her room remained untouched until she could one day return.

Two stewardesses smiled wide as they welcomed her aboard and the pilot introduced himself with a polite royal address.

She entered the plush interior of the plane and a sickening jolt went through her once she sat down, looking out of the window. She'd never been on a plane, never even left Florida. This was her first ride on a roller coaster magnified about a thousand times.

Gabby longed for reassurance as she sat down, but didn't want to seem like the giant baby she felt inside.

She casually looked out of her window, the loud airplane engine making it seem as though she would be launched into space. Perhaps they would sit here for the next hour. Perhaps customs would take their time inspecting them.

She couldn't tell if she was more worried that she would get this close, only to be denied due to her missing passport, or that they would let her go anyway. It seemed irresponsible of them to do that. Federal stuff like that wasn't so lax in her limited experience.

Suddenly the door was shut. As if no one was coming to check their passports. No one seemed to find it odd. One of the flight attendants started up the short aisle. Gabby reached out to grab her arm at the cuff.

"Excuse me, but... what's going on?" Gabby asked.

"My Queen?"

"I thought customs was going to check us."

"They will let us leave. Not to worry," the king cut through their conversation.

Gabby squinted. Something seemed funny.

She looked to Max, who seemed adamant about not making eye contact. The two men equally refused to look at each other as if guilt-stricken.

She got a bad feeling in the pit of her stomach as her mind brought a heartbreaking detail to the fore: Don't you have to take pictures for a passport?

Why couldn't she have thought of this days before now? Hours?

She swallowed. She surveyed the plush interior of the plane that may as well have been a white van.

"Let me off," she heard herself blurt.

The two men didn't move. The two stewardesses simply looked at each other. Her pulse going up and up with no signs of falling.

Finally, Max turned to face her. "Why, Princess?"

"Something's not right. And I don't feel comfortable with this," she insisted, unbuckling her seatbelt, her head not the only thing shaking. "Nothing is happening like you said."

"Princess Asha..."

"I don't know how they do things in your country, but I don't feel comfortable breaking the law by leaving the U.S. If I just got my visa approved, I want to stay above board. I don't understand why you can't just wait a bit longer—"

"My Queen, with all due respect, you are talking crazy," the king said.

Max stiffened. As did Gabby.

"Excuse me?"

"We don't have time for this," said Mazigh out loud. Emir could only look ahead remorsefully.

"What is this?" she asked, looking back and forth between them when they didn't answer. "Is this... are you kidnapping me?"

Max took a breath. "Gabby—"

"Don't *Gabby* me. Who *are* you?"

She looked over at the king, who looked out of the window as though nothing was happening. Suddenly she felt the plane slowly start to move.

Her heart took off faster than any plane. Gabby turned her attention to Max, the one who'd shown her the citizenship papers. The booklet.

The plane was moving and it dawned on her. The papers were fake. There was no passport.

They had done nothing. Nothing but make her an accessory. Gabby was still without a country.

"You said you had connections. You said... that they had an office in Florida."

"That part was true."

"That *part*?" she scoffed. "I don't understand. I thought you were honorable."

"Your father's Ashwari was part of a war that Manaf's allies fought against," the king broke in. "The King can still get your country back, but we have to move quickly. I wish we had more time to get you what you want."

"You could've just said that," Gabby breathed angrily.

"There was no pleasant way to do this. Either approach would've ended the same," Max appealed.

"So you pretended I had a choice in this. Ignorant American girl."

"You did have a choice, Princess."

"Don't get me wrong, I'm impressed. Those papers," Gabby shook her head. "They were so *real*. I wanted them to be real."

Max got out of his seat and toddled across the aisle as the plane inched along the runway. He knelt down in front of her chair and Gabby froze, feeling strange. It was unexpected and somehow seemed like something he would never do. He still looked quite large while on his knees, like a lion suddenly coming up to her to be petted. He took her hand again and suddenly she couldn't think.

"They don't even know that you're here, my Queen," Max began sympathetically. "So why cause an international incident by telling them?"

Tears gathered in her eyes as she processed what he was telling her.

She exploded her own leverage the moment they met, telling them plainly that she was undocumented. So they lied. She was never free and never would be. She was nothing but a pawn in some international game.

What else about this supposedly equally beneficial plan were they not telling her? Would she ever see her family again?

"Get me off of this plane right now."

"My Queen, you are not safe here. Your own family knows

that."

"Oh, and I'm safer with two lying kidnappers?"

"We were afraid of this. We didn't want to alarm you."

"Great job!" Gabby cried. "And just what would you have done? If I hadn't agreed to any of it?"

"Anything that was in the King's power to do, Princess," the king spoke up behind them, clearly exasperated.

Max felt Gabby stiffen under his hands. His jaw clenched.

Foolish Mazigh. The princess was still under the impression that he was her future husband. If this was him doing an impression, then he needed to pull back.

Gabby abruptly relinquished Max's hand, breathing hard. She got out of her seat and started moving to the back of the plane. With each arm extended, she sought an anchor in every direction and looked to and fro out of the small windows, as if finding a way to jump out at the plane's low speed toward the runway.

Max grabbed her arm, trying gently to subdue her. "Princess, you must stay seated for takeoff."

"I want to go home," she cried, hysterical. "*Ema! Ema!*"

She wriggled in his grasp until they each felt the plane come to a stop at the base of the runway.

He grabbed her middle and had no choice but to hold the Princess Asha to him on his lap as the plane picked up speed.

He couldn't see her face as she cried out again and again for her *Ema*. And he barely made out her sobs of anguish over the roar of the plane as the plane began to ascend.

He'd never been so close to the Princess, had hardly touched her outside of a gesture or a helping hand. Had he been in his home country, he would've hardly been allowed that before the wedding day.

Now she was against him and he was smelling her smells,

feeling her slight body against him light as a feather. And as much as he wanted to savor it, all he wanted to do was crawl into a hole and never come out.

* * *

Princess Asha cried herself to sleep after about an hour, a relief to King Khoury and his vizier.

It was the second time during this trip that he was unsure of himself. The first time was on the way there. Sitting in the very chair he was in now. Feeling rather silly to be traveling across the world on behalf of a rumor.

Mazigh said the reports back home were already speculating about them since the press could confirm Bel's private plane had left for America with the King of Manaf on it.

Still, when he arrived at the little house and saw the knowledge in the mother's face, the feeling was palpable and gave him hope. Laying eyes on Princess Asha the first time made him frightened by the possibility of being wrong. The test results from her parents did the rest.

He should have just stuck to the original plan. He planned for a fight. Planned to take covert measures and simply have her wake up in the air. Quiet, clean. Illegal, but then so was she.

She would be sore about for a while. But she would adjust. Just like him. Her life was not her own, as she mistakenly believed. This could be the bond their relationship would be built on.

He didn't expect her to pragmatically strike a compromise. He didn't expect her to be so prepared to hear the truth about her blood. She had, in fact, been waiting. Whether she knew it or not.

He gave her time. Enough time to acclimate to the knowledge.

She got to pack and work and speak reasonably with the ones she was forced to go with. She got to eat dinner and say goodbye to her father.

So why did he feel almost feverish with guilt?

Though it was better that everyone be confused about his time in America, the remorse sifted through his thought process, finding all the places he could've leveled with her.

Silly childhood games. He didn't want to admit to himself how much he wanted to keep driving around all day in a strange land with a strange girl, as no one but a stranger himself.

He could never love a place like America, but Bel was right. It was dangerously seductive indeed.

There was no other choice, he convinced himself. If he hadn't pretended to be the vizier he would've had to leave Asha out of his sight. Even worse, she'd be left with Mazigh, who couldn't help turning on the charm. Especially when he wasn't supposed to.

"*I trust that you have a plan, my King,*" his vizier switched to Arabic, breaking the silence.

The King turned his head to Mazigh as he took his time answering, still sore about his poor judgment from earlier.

"Oddly, I don't," the King finally replied.

"How do you mean?"

"Just what I said, Mazigh."

"I cannot deceive the Princess any longer," Mazigh shook his head. "I quit."

"You must."

"Why? The worst of it is over. Why can't you just reveal who you are once she wakes up?"

"I will not have my marriage begin with this bitterness."

Mazigh raised his eyebrows and rubbed his face as though

dealing with a crazy man. King Khoury let it slide. Because there was a possibility that he was crazy.

But Gabby confided in Max, relaxed with him.

He was confident that with Max's help, he could turn this around in a day or two. In time for the wedding. He thought he could at least put off her inevitable hatred for him.

But if there was a shot that she wouldn't have to hate him at all, he should take it. He hoped once she landed in beautiful Manaf, she would forget all about this wretched country of hers.

"Just how will we pull this off?"

"The Ashwari doctor managed well enough. Our staff would be no different. Saad knows of the games we used to play, he will explain. Most of them would not need to know anyway. We keep the Princess confined to the palace as she normally would be. The language barrier will work to our advantage."

"And what will I do?"

"Relax, Mazigh. You will keep your distance, as expected. Your job is practically done."

"It will be unusual for you to have so much access to the Princess before the wedding. As for me, I will look like a slacker."

"These are unusual circumstances, everyone will understand. Also, I am the King. What I say is normal is normal."

"I'm not worried about those at *home*, your Majesty, I am worried about her. Finding out before you can tell her. The binding ceremony," Mazigh remembered.

King Khoury frowned. "Nothing has to change. We are separated the entire day."

"You really plan on letting this go on that long?"

"No. Only a few days. And then she'll know."

"She'll be ambushed."

"She already has been," the King replied sympathetically.

"She just lost everything. Because of me. Let her adjust."

"Is this really about her adjusting?"

The King sighed, losing patience. "What do you mean, Mazigh?"

"We both know she fancies you, not me."

"Which is why I am confident in continuing the charade."

"Why not reveal your true identity so that she can be comforted with one good outcome of this?"

The King looked over at Gabby's delicate sleeping visage.

"Today I imagine she will refuse to be comforted," he lamented. "Just follow my lead."

* * *

The King and future Queen arrived first in Ghassan. They'd chased the sun all night until it was the following afternoon. Now they were returning the private jet back to its owner.

King Belkacem and his wife, Queen Kimberly awaited them on the tarmac at King Khoury's request. Gabby had hardly spoken or eaten during the twelve-hour flight. Emir feared she might make a break for it as soon as they landed. He thought she should be comforted by some American faces.

The King and his Queen were surrounded by a small entourage, King Bel in his suit and Queen Kimberly in a billowy, European-inspired saree, her wavy hair loose under her headdress with long strands blown by the wind. It was late at night, so he would only have to worry about the most diligent of paparazzi with the most expensive of telephoto lenses.

King Khoury and Mazigh exited the plane first alone. With the help of the flight attendants and looking dazed, Gabby exited the plane behind them, wearing a simple blouse and jeans she'd packed in the streamlined luggage that made up the sum total of her possessions.

She was introduced to Bel and she relinquished an exhausted smile. When she was introduced to Queen Kimberly, however, she instantly broke down crying.

Kim was undeterred. Having been briefed on the situation beforehand, the Queen put one arm around her, turned, and whisked her away without a word.

The three men watched as the two queens made their way to the caravan of vehicles escorting them the short distance back to the Ghassani palace, a train of ladies-in-waiting their caboose.

"*I take it you decided on the tranquilizer,*" Bel assumed in Farsi as he turned from the sight to look back at King Khoury.

"Actually, we came up with a worse plan, Your Majesty," Mazigh interjected.

"Do I want to know?"

"I'm afraid it's necessary that you do," Emir sighed.

* * *

Queen Kimberly snuck in bed next to her husband a few hours after King Khoury's arrival, having stayed up with Gabby until she'd calmed enough to sleep.

"How is she?" Bel mumbled.

"She's so cute, oh my God," Kim let out a sigh like she'd been holding it in until Bel asked.

"Everything okay?"

"She'll be fine. Just a little shaken up," Kim said, undressing. "She's just like I was. Never been outside of the state let alone the country, never even been on a plane and now she's deadass in a whoooole new world. Fuckin' magic carpet rides and some

117

mo' shit."

"Damn," Bel sympathized with his eyes closed.

"Her family's the complete opposite of mine. Had a lot less time to say goodbye than I did. But she'll be fine."

"Hmm..." he sleepily replied. A few seconds went by until Kim brought up the following concern.

"But apparently, somebody thought it was okay for her to spend all her waking hours with Mazigh? She said he told her to call him Max. Yeah... I don't think Mazigh would do anything sketchy, but... she must've said his name like fifty times. I mean... I know they're supposed to apart before the wedding and all that, but that's no fuckin' bueno."

Bel gave her a drowsy, delayed response. "Ohhh, yeah no, Max is Emir."

"How's that?"

"They did some *Coming to America* shit when they got there. So she thinks Mazigh's the king, and now they don't know how to switch it back."

Kim overlooked the crazy thing Bel had just described to focus on the obvious.

"How do they not know how? I'm pretty sure, 'hey, sike, I'm the King' would work.

"I know, but I think he's just got the jitters."

Kim raised an eyebrow. "He got the jitters?"

"Yeah. I mean I get it. Growing up a royal, you never know who *actually* wants to fuck with you. I grew up in the palace, but him? He's been King aaaaaallll his life, basically. He got to the U.S. and just like that, it was all a dream. He's enjoying the anonymity."

"He's lucky he didn't get fuckin' shot."

"What you said," Bel mumbled. "Plus, you know he's a little

intense. He's super in love with her already and it's making him do all the wrong shit, you know how it goes."

"Awwwwwmy God I'm gonna diieeeee!" Kim fake cried over their secret fake affair. "So... what did you tell him to do?"

"About..."

"About how to come clean."

"Nothin'."

"NOthin'??" Kim repeated, outraged. "So when is she supposed to find out?"

"Wedding day, I guess," Bel shrugged, slightly frustrated that Kim was still talking. One more minute and he was gonna be up for good. "Shit's goin' down Saturday, I told 'em we'll see him there."

"Lord ha'mmercy... did *you* tell him to do that?"

"What? The *Coming to America* shit?"

"Yeah."

"I told him nothing."

"This wedding about to be entertaining AF," Kim mused.

Bel was just about to drift off to sleep when Kim whisper-blurted, "I am very happy to be here!"

Bel couldn't be annoyed as he giggled at Kim's accurate assessment of Emir's trip.

10

Chapter 10

It was a short forty-five-minute drive from the Ghassani palace to Manaf. King Belkacem hosted them overnight after their tedious journey, fed them in the morning, and sent them home in a single car at King Khoury's request. All while the King and Queen of Ghassan slept the morning away per their usual routine on Thursdays.

It took two days, but Princess Asha finally agreed to eat.

Emir had her watched around the clock. There were two more days until the wedding and he was worried she would waste away. Her frame was already slight, to begin with.

He also found himself unable to eat, too full of guilt and lies. She'd declined offers to see the king *or* Max. He commanded that someone notify him the moment she'd requested food.

When the moment came, he'd been in a council meeting with Mazigh and five of his most trusted advisors about how to reveal the Queen's royal bloodline.

"The country is abuzz with the news that you may have found love while in America."

King Khoury sat at the head of the long mahogany table, excitement at a low rumble inside him. The reports, for once, were true. He knew because he'd been away from her for 36 hours and it was unbearable.

"How did the King do, Mazigh?" Saad asked. He was the King's oldest advisor, his father's old driver.

"You wouldn't believe me if I told you," Mazigh teased with a grave look. The room dared a titter while the King looked sternly on.

"I'm sorry our friends at the consulate couldn't be more of use with the paperwork," another advisor spoke up.

Mazigh dismissed his concern. "The notice was short. What they pulled off was beyond the call."

"No one suspects her identity?" the King asked.

"No. They believe that the King of Ghassan influenced you to find an American bride."

The King nodded, satisfied that gossip had provided a better cover than secrecy.

"Excellent. Do not correct them. We will present the Queen after the ceremony and not before."

"Your Majesty, I do not think it's safe to expose her to crowds once her true lineage is revealed."

King Khoury sickened at the thought of General Olayinka sending assassins, which he would most certainly do.

But presenting her before the wedding meant revealing his own identity to her sooner rather than later.

"Cancel it entirely," the King said.

"...Yes, my King."

"Do you object?"

"No, my King. This would mark the first time, perhaps in the history of the country, that we did not present a new Queen, but the circumstances are unique. Perhaps the people will understand."

"We will have a banquet once Olayinka is neutralized."

"Of course, your Majesty."

Suddenly, one of the Queen's maids had been permitted entry. The council table looked confused and put out. Equally, the woman seemed to be second-guessing the command she was given.

"Your Majesty? The... Queen has requested lunch."

King Khoury nodded and got up from his seat. "Thank you. Gentleman, excuse me."

The council only looked at each other. Even after explaining the extraordinary circumstances of having to see her so much before the binding ceremony, they couldn't quite understand what was so important about the Princess's lunch.

"If this is a sign of what's to come, I don't know if I like the American Queen," said Taik, his highest-ranked General.

"If I would have bet my life's earnings that King Khoury would be the last man who could be swayed by feminine wiles, I would have lost that bet, wouldn't I?" smiled Saad.

"Queen consort Asha is a natural beauty as her mother was. Emir is particular but not superhuman," Mazigh reminded them.

"Everyone here knows this. But he has had women presented to him since he came of age. Younger, more suitable women," another advisor voiced.

"Women who assumed their beauty and breeding would be enough. But how many of them have also lost their father the King because of others' pursuit of power?" Mazigh pointed out with sympathy. "I have spent some time with the girl and I understand. The King wants someone who will understand him.

"

"He breaks tradition to attend to her and they are not yet married. This is concerning."

Mazigh answered curtly. "It is Olayinka who causes our traditions to be broken. And Princess Asha has agreed to lose her traditions entirely. He is merely meeting her some of the way."

The advisors hushed at Mazigh's impassioned defense. All but one.

"These circumstances are extraordinary," one bravely reiterated.

"The King is aware. But he's also aware that the King will decide what is extraordinary. You would do well to remember that."

Everyone looked to Saad, the only one entrusted to continue.

"We have no choice, then. We're counting on you to talk sense into him, Mazigh. Your loyalty to your friend must not outweigh that of Manaf."

Mazigh let his face soften, empathetic to the room. A strange young woman had come in and exerted more control over the King in a day than most of them had combined. They had not had a hand in choosing her. She was a wild card.

"You mustn't overreact. The King isn't new to many things, but he is new to this. You have nothing to worry about. You'll see."

* * *

Princess Asha woke up, not remembering how she fell asleep, or how she ended up in bed completely undressed and under the covers.

She must've cried herself to sleep. And her attendants had tucked her comfortably in bed. Sneaky little ghosts. There was no other explanation.

The Queen consort hadn't wanted any company when she arrived in Manaf, but she was grateful to her ladies-in-waiting for making it virtually impossible for her to be alone. She didn't speak Arabic and yet they could decipher what she needed. They smiled whenever she looked their way, ready to serve.

"Some tea, my Queen. To help you sleep," one of her attendants offered the night before. She'd broken the ice while Princess Asha sat wordlessly in the Queen's study and brought her a steaming, ornate cup full. It was strong and floral and instantly gave her strength after she'd refused food the entire day.

She brought Gabby another cup the next morning without being asked. She spoke the Queen's English and was the one who translated between her and the rest of the girls. She seemed to be the leader. Her name was Zara.

"So is it true what they say, your Majesty?" Zara asked.

"What do they say?" the Queen answered back.

"That the King asked for your hand as soon as he saw you?"

"More or less," Gabby replied.

It wasn't a lie. But she assumed her full identity was still concealed.

"How wonderful," Zara lowered her head and smiled in awe. She seemed as though she'd been bursting to ask that since she got there. "Is it true your family is from Ashwari, your Majesty?"

Wow. People really were discussing her. "It is."

"What is America like, your Majesty?"

"Uh... well... it's... I don't know. Cool. I've never been outside of the country until now."

"My apologies, my Queen, if I am too casual with you. I am new to royal service."

"So am I," Gabby smiled.

"Do you not find the King handsome?"

Gabby's smile lessened a bit. "I do," she simply answered.

"He's been that way since he was a boy. *Malik Shab*, the boy King, was his nickname. Every girl in Manaf grew up hoping to marry him one day."

"What about Mazigh?" Gabby harmlessly asked.

"What about him, my Queen?"

"He is also handsome, is he not?"

"He is," Zara conceded. "Not much is known about him. But no one is closer to the King than he is."

"Believe me, I've noticed," Gabby dared a raw tone of resentment. "I've spent more time with him than I have the man I'm supposed to be marrying."

"It's Manafi tradition that the bride be kept away from the groom until after the binding ceremony. We are not so modern as the West when it comes to values. The father of the groom still pays the bride price in some parts of Manaf. Your relationship will change overnight once the two of you are wed."

"To be honest, I'm a bit afraid of that," Gabby divulged, trying to imagine the King's hands on her bare skin, his lips on her lips.

She kept thinking of his stern dismissal of her distress on the plane. How could she ever be vulnerable at all in front of him again?

"Afraid, my Queen?"

"You might say that I'm a bit more inexperienced than most, Zara."

"As in... have you never... been with a man, your Majesty?"

"I have not."

"Good answer, my Queen," Zara winked. Gabby laughed. She was liking this gal more and more. She reminded her of her sister.

"I know it sounds ridiculous, but it's true, unfortunately."

"Then you must be very nervous indeed."

"I just wish I knew the King more before we... I wish we had an opportunity to... connect. First."

"It's... understandable if you are getting 'cold feet' as they say, my Queen."

Gabby stiffened. Zara obviously didn't know anything about her being kidnapped. Why would she? And now she all but admitted that she felt nothing for the King.

"I'm not, it's just... I guess I didn't anticipate how hard it would be to leave everything I knew to come here."

"I gathered that, my Queen," Zara nodded, collecting her empty teacup. "My mother also left her home to marry my father."

"Did it ever get better?"

Zara nodded. "Once she was pregnant. She grew to love my father, of course, but... she always said having me gave her a new sense of what home really was."

From the south-facing window, Asha could see a cluster of builders on the beach efficiently constructing a large pergola made from beautiful reddish wood gleaming in the sunlight. Likely preparations for the ceremony in just a few days. She'd been terribly jetlagged and wasn't sure what day it was already. She sighed, suppressing the less than thrilled mood coming over her.

She was angry at the King for misleading her. The last thing she needed was this hurdle of trust plaguing an already fledgling relationship. Why isn't he helping himself?

She got the feeling that he didn't care about her at all. That it was all a ruse to get her here, to get Ashwari in his possession. Another one of her sighs echoed through the large space.

Her room was as long as it was high. It had a huge four-post bed on one end and a sitting room on the other. The large windows overlooked the capital below which descended in every direction into jagged ancient narrow avenues, the vivid cerulean of the sea visible at the end of each one. The palace of Manaf sat atop a large hill. Unlike Ghassan, Manaf's terrain was diverse, especially along the coast. A natural barrier from would-be raiders.

Hints of a distant, unnamed European influence were everywhere, from the architecture to the clothing, which seemed to mesh the colors and culture of the east with the medieval influences of the west.

Outside of her room was an open staircase below. A glass dome lit the corridor by day. Instead of her floor being lined with rooms, there was an open dining room and another sitting area across the spiraling balcony. The entire floor was essentially hers.

"My Queen," her attendants bowed as they followed her movements toward the door, realizing she was trying to leave her room. One of them hastily reached for the knob and several more of them went ahead of her. She smiled.

"Mackenzie's not gonna believe this," she laughed. Though she didn't know when her family would be permitted to visit, she consoled herself with the idea that they soon would.

Her food was brought to her at the long dining table. The large wooden pocket doors were currently open.

"*Everyone upstairs*," she suddenly heard in Zara's Arabic. Asha watched her attendants scamper wordlessly for the hallway, bowing slightly as they walked past the King's guard, unseen on the other side.

Zara bowed once slow and low before leaving the doorway and Max appeared in her place. The doors were kept open.

"My Queen," he said, nearly choked up at the sight of her. He hadn't seen her in days and already she looked transformed in a billowy tunic made of burgundy, navy, and golds. She had gold on her wrists, and her hair was smooth and long. Her smoky makeup brought out her Ethiopian mother's features. No hair was out of place. She looked like a born royal.

Gabby failed to stifle her smile at the sight of Max grinning and looking thrilled to be back in his own country.

"You look like a pig in shit, Max," were the first words she'd spoken to him since they left the U.S.

The curse word stung his ears like smooth bourbon. She seemed to be in good spirits.

"If you mean that I am happy to be home, then you are right," he said as he sat down next to her at the head of the small table.

"What brings you here?"

"I was told you requested lunch. I thought I would join you."

The Queen rolled her eyes a bit, self-consciously. "Someone really bothered you about that?"

"The King has commanded to be briefed on your every move, my Queen. He laments over what happened. He wishes you weren't so unhappy here."

"I'm not unhappy here. It's beautiful. I'm enchanted by it, really," Asha looked around, her bored visage betraying her words. She sighed. "I apologize for my outburst. On the plane."

"No need."

"The King must think he has agreed to marry a child."

"Nonsense. He sympathizes with your grief."

"He seemed annoyed with me."

"He can be a bit... coarse. But he doesn't know his own strength sometimes."

"You can stop covering for him, Max. He thinks I'm a fool."

"He doesn't. He's simply impatient. His plan before we left here was to shoot you with a tranquilizer dart and simply haul you away without anyone being the wiser."

"What?!"

"Thankfully, I talked him out of it."

"Well, I suppose I should thank you, then. For giving me the chance to say goodbye..." a tear welled up in her eye.

Before he knew what was happening he'd reached out and caught it at her chin with his fingers.

Gabby leaned into his touch and he tried to ignore it as they locked eyes. At least he'd gotten her mind off of their blunders. For the moment.

Tell her now.

"Try to be strong," he said. "For me. It's selfish, I know. I have a distaste in seeing you cry. Especially when I'm the cause."

"You? How is it your fault?"

Tell. Her. Now.

"...I don't know," he said.

"We're a lot alike, you and me," the Queen suddenly said.

"How so?"

"We're duty-bound. To a fault. And we like it. Of course, mine is only a week old."

"So you do want to be here?"

"Of course. Manaf is more beautiful than anything I could've ever imagined..." Asha's voice trailed off as she sat back in her chair.

The lump in her throat was unbearable and she couldn't

control her self-pity. Her ineffable emotions contorted her face and tears again blurred her eyes.

He didn't want to make her uncomfortable, but he couldn't hold himself back when she cried. So far, it was only ever because of something he had done.

She fell silent as he inched closer towards her, as he had at the restaurant. He opened his posture with an arm relaxed behind her on the chair, inviting her to his arms.

He didn't seem worried at all about the appearance of it, but she unconsciously hesitated. Obviously, it was innocent for him. She took one glance at the open door of her study before she let herself accept his invitation.

Against his gentle, yet sturdy chest she stood virtually no chance. She cried all the more, which seemed to fluster him. His arms enveloped her shoulders and she felt her head resting in the crook of his neck.

He was almost positive if he told her the truth right now, she would be relieved. He couldn't replace her family, but knowing she would be marrying him instead of Mazigh might be enough.

"I'm sorry," she said, interrupting his thoughts. "I know what I signed up for, and I do want this. More than anything, I just... I'll adjust," she sniffed, trying not to snot all over his white linen shirt.

"Why do you say that?"

"Say what?"

"That you want this more than anything?" he asked, his chin atop her head.

Gabby quieted, trying to think of something rational to answer with. He was holding her so secure and she'd never been held before by someone as big as him, who wasn't related to her.

"I don't know why I said that," she sniffed, his chest muffling her voice. "I just know that it's true."

To know that she wanted this more than anything eased his conscience. He imagined that she knew she was his destiny just as much as he knew it, felt it, on the way to her.

"Gabby, I—"

"I'm just so angry," she whispered.

That surprised him. "At whom?" he urged her.

"Everyone. Myself. The King. You. My parents."

He knew it.

"You mustn't hold bitterness toward your parents. They made the right decision. They couldn't have known the King's plan to smuggle you back to Manaf."

"No, my real parents. For how it happened. I'm angry at both of them. If my father hadn't been so paranoid he wouldn't have forced my mother to come home. If my mother had just waited a few weeks, she could've claimed asylum and stayed. She could've been safe."

Max empathized. It was a familiar game of hindsight that he knew all too well. It seemed productive at first, but only led down a path of madness.

"Your mother was never safe," Max replied stoically. "Olayinka would've never rolled out his plan until your mother returned. Thank your father's paranoia for forcing everyone in the palace to pretend their marriage was intact, and that you were there. I have no doubt that your mother died with relieved hope, and your father went to his death with glee in his heart, that he'd bested his treacherous general. It is the kind of Ace in the hole that every king dreams of having at that moment."

His raw speech made her feel oddly better. To think of her parents having hope in their final moments because of her jolted her right out of her self-pity.

She understood. It would've happened how it happened.

Gabby nodded against him, holding onto his chest like a toddler on her first day of pre-school. He smelled like sandalwood and leather. And now she had smells to add to her forbidden fantasies that she'd swore to never again entertain.

Finally, she let go, not wanting to appear forlorn as she was to leave his embrace. She quickly dabbed her eyes, changing the subject.

"My attendants tell me I'm in for a long day tomorrow."

"Indeed. The binding ceremony."

"This isn't named for anything nefarious is it?"

"No. From what I've been told, the bride is celebrated the entire day. But it does have the reputation of being dull."

"I wish my family could be here."

"After the formalities are over with, you may have as many ceremonies as you want. I promise."

"How can you promise that?"

Shit. Shit. Shit.

"The King mentioned having a second ceremony after the first. For the people," Max recovered.

"The people?"

"The King traditionally presents his Queen in a public ceremony before the wedding."

"Like Ghassan did."

"Precisely. The King has postponed his until after Olayinka can be neutralized."

"...Because someone might try to kill me??" the Queen deduced.

"The King is merely taking every precaution," he put her at ease.

"But no one knows who I am yet. If it's for the people of Manaf, tell the King I'm more than happy to keep the tradition."

Max left out the part about it being scheduled for today.

He had a brief thought that he could've gotten away with having Mazigh come out on the balcony with them as well... nah, that wouldn't have worked.

"You are generous, my Queen, but it has already been decided. The King will hold a great banquet in your honor once you are wed. I'm sure that he would do the same once your family is safe to visit."

"It's a nice gesture, but I've never been one to parade myself around just so my family could watch. I would want them here for moral support. To hold my hand. They're my security blanket, I suppose. I've never not had them."

"I understand, my Queen."

Asha bit her lip and launched into her poorly disguised anxieties. "Apparently, the next time I see the King it will be under the wedding canopy. When we're husband and wife."

"That is true, my Queen."

"Do *you* think I'm overreacting, Mazigh?"

"Call me Max."

"But your real name is so beautiful."

"More beautiful than Emir?" he jealously teased.

"I'm not allowed to call the King by his name."

"Nor will I allow you to call me by mine."

Asha got up from her place at the table slowly walked past Max, towards the open balcony.

"One day, Mazigh, you will love a woman. And she'll be allowed to say your beautiful name. Because you're not the King. And you'll be glad of it. You'll want her to."

Max's tongue stuck to the roof of his mouth as he casually followed behind, fighting the urge to slink his arm around her diminutive waist.

"I'm starting to envy you, Max. All the perks of being the man in charge without the rules and regulations. Why haven't you found love yet?" She asked as he leaned with one arm on the thick stone ledge beside her.

"As soon as I discover the reason, you will be the first to know."

"Is his mother even really from Ashwari?" she turned to him.

"My Queen?"

"His mother. Or did you tell me that just to get me to go?"

"Have you spent time on your terrace, my Queen?"

"No, honestly."

"The King was strategic in choosing your room," he said, pointing. "Look over there."

Beyond the view of the city below, was a body of water in the distance, presumed to be the Arabian Sea. Beyond that was a distant red and gray cluster of a town, yet it was close enough to see the bustle of boats along the coast. No skyscrapers, no towers, not even trees. A heatwave blurred in front of it.

"Is that.... Ashwari?"

"It is. The King's mother was indeed born there."

"And his father?"

"The Khoury line is indigenous to Manaf."

She shielded the sun from her eyes and looked at it in wonder. "Can we go there?"

"To Ashwari?" he chuckled. "You will, my Queen."

"When?"

"Soon. Once the King has you under his protection."

"You mean once he has acquired Ashwari through marriage."

"Princess..."

"I appreciate his thoughtful room choice in his beautiful

palace, but I'm not under any illusions. This is a prison cell."

"The incident on the plane has turned you cynical, my Queen."

"And you are here to placate the prisoner."

"I came of my own volition."

"Really."

"Yes."

"Why?"

"To see you."

Asha's eyes averted to the water below them. "The King may not think much of that."

"The king has more important things to do than monitor his advisor's every move."

"Why did you come?" She prompted. "Of your own volition?"

"Because the King is concerned about you wasting away days before the wedding."

Asha nodded once, remaining stoic. "The King is lucky to have someone that can be concerned for him in his absence."

His stupid plan was having the unintended consequence of making the King into a ruthless, unfeeling cad.

"I must reiterate, it is not customary for the King to—"

"Like, I said. I'm under no illusions. You don't have to cover for him. Really. I know why I agreed to come here. And it wasn't for romance. The King has been honest with me on that front, and for that, I respect him. That will be enough. I've never known romance, so I'm not sad about what I'll be missing. Besides, I doubt it can compete with looking out over the water at land and people that are yours to govern."

"You'd be surprised, my Queen," Max replied. But Gabby was still looking out at the water, ignoring his attentions on her, his close proximity. She wished he would leave already. And yet, the thought sickened her.

135

"How could such a small piece of land warrant all this... strategy?"

"A country is not merely its physical size. It is its people, location, its resources, its political significance. Ashwari represents the interests of the five nations that surround it, who ultimately represent the interests of Iran," he said. "It is the cornerstone in East African affairs. Just a stone's throw away. The eyes of the Middle East are upon it."

Just then, she had an epiphany. An exciting one.

"Max, I need you to say yes to what I'm about to ask you."

Yes, he thought.

"I'll do my best."

"I want to request another audience with the King."

Chapter 11

Max frowned. He couldn't say yes to that.

He should've anticipated this. Now was his chance. She could show up to find him in the King's chamber, on his throne. And all would be revealed.

A bizarre scene played out in his mind, where Gabby just refused to believe anything anymore and had to be carried off by his guards after he'd embarrassed her himself.

"My Queen... the wedding is two days away," he reasoned.

"Which is why it can't wait."

Max wet his lips, thinking of a kind way to shut her down. "Princess Asha—"

"What I have to say hinges on me showing up on Saturday. Tell him I'll consider it a wedding present," she said with a tone of seductiveness. At least to him.

He sighed. He was her champion, the one she trusted, and she wanted him to go to bat for her. She could've been using him, using their growing rapport against him, but he couldn't fault her. He was the only source of leverage she had in this place. If she only knew it was all she would ever need.

"I'll see what I can do," Max promised, as he turned to leave the Queen on the terrace.

"Will you not be staying for lunch?" she asked with her back turned, still facing Ashwari.

Max stopped short, a stifled grin activating one of his dimples. Guilt and flattery warred as he thought of a vizier-like response.

"If the Queen wants an audience with the King, I'll have to act quickly."

"Very well," she dismissed him after a long pause.

Hours later her attendants were taking her to the King's court. She got a little intimidated as she passed the empty throne room as big as a theater, and was escorted into the private chamber. Max opened the outer door and the Queen made her way inside, the king sitting on top of his massive desk instead of behind it.

"Wait here," Max quietly said to her maids, shutting them out. Once it was just the three of them, Gabby turned to the king, who gave her a swift smile that seemed to her impatient.

"You look radiant, Princess Asha. Welcome to your new home. How are you enjoying Manaf?"

"Your vizier calls me Queen, your Majesty."

"Does he now?"

"He does. As do my attendants." The Queen looked over at Max who wore a discouraging poker face.

"My vizier takes liberties," the king said. "In the eyes of the law, you will be a queen once you are accepted by the King in the presence of witnesses on your wedding day."

"I am still the rightful Queen of Ashwari."

"Ashwari is currently under military rule."

"Semantics."

"Which I believe are important."

"It's funny you say that your Majesty because it pertains

somewhat to why I'm here."

"I eagerly await the point of this visit, Princess."

"I want Ashwari to become independent."

In the room there was a pregnant pause, during which Max thought he probably should've found out what the Queen wanted to ask before they got there.

And he was also relieved that he hadn't picked this moment to reveal himself. Otherwise, he would have to take the impending heat of telling the Queen "no," which he wasn't in the mood to do.

The king made a show of slowly pacing behind his large desk. Max stood behind the Queen, so she couldn't see him rolling his eyes.

"Naturally, you would," the king finally said.

"Naturally?"

"Yes. You just left America behind. Naturally, you would want to re-create it in your backyard. But the King cannot simply install democracies as a wedding present."

The Queen's heart rate quickened a bit. "It amuses me that you say I 'left America behind,' your Majesty. When I was misled."

"Are you admitting that if we had not given in to your impossible demands to gain, in a matter of hours, citizenship to a country you would no longer be living in, you would not have taken the offer?"

"We'll never know, my King. Because you chose to lie," the Queen held her own. "I've held up my end of the bargain, while your end slowly disintegrated to nothing once you returned to your home. I'm giving you a chance to regain my trust and affection."

"By upsetting at least a half dozen African nations?"

"I'm not here representing the others. I'm here on behalf of

Ashwari."

"And I can respect that, Princess. But with all due respect, seeing a country from your balcony does not a representative make."

Max cringed. The Queen remained undeterred.

"I know enough to understand that the common people have had enough of being ruled. Ashwari has only known tyranny for a half-century."

"By way of despots, yes, of course."

"...Despots like my father?" Asha filled in.

"Precisely," the king retorted without hesitation.

The Queen only stared back chillingly. Oh boy. This was not going well.

"Princess Asha, I can appreciate that this trip has made you... emotional. Being so close to your ancestral home has endowed you with a newfound patriotism, and that pleases me."

Max tried to jump in. "Perhaps his majesty the king—"

"But Manaf has enjoyed prosperity and stability since the King was a child. Do you insult your King by lumping his exemplary leadership in with dictators? I'm sympathetic to your connection to Ashwari's former king, but he was no man to admire."

"And yet I've heard no stories of how he had to kidnap his love interests."

Ohh, shit.

The king was so taken aback he couldn't hold back his huff of a laugh. It really was a good thing for her that none of this was real.

He looked over at Max, who must've been thinking the same. He slowly raised his eyebrows in admiration of the insult, indirectly meant for him.

The king let a gleaming smile escape defensively and Max got a bad feeling. He knew what someone pretending to be the king would have to do to save face right now.

"Come now, Princess, you are beautiful and all, but rest assured—"

"I think what the Princess has proposed has merit. Your majesty," Max desperately interjected.

Tension crackled in the room between the two men.

Even Gabby noticed that Max had interrupted the king. A beat or two went by as they all stood stock still.

"Please excuse us, Princess?" the king said without looking up.

Gabby was almost afraid to leave Max alone, but she knew that was silly. As she opened the door with her attendants on the other side, Max bellowed hastily, "take the Queen back to her chamber."

The Queen looked back but didn't speak as her attendants bowed and rushed her away without a word.

He was grateful for their silence of omission as the door closed behind them. He'd paraded his little game around in front of the Queen's servants a few times now and Queen Asha hadn't been the wiser.

Emir let the silence linger a bit, knowing he was in a little trouble. He'd put his friend in an awkward position.

"I didn't know she was going to ask that, by the way," Max said. The king remained quiet.

"This little impression of me you're doing is setting me back one whole week," Max only half-joked.

"Are you out of your mind?" Mazigh asked. "I need to know if the Princess has broken your mind. Because I told the council they had nothing to worry about."

"They are worried? About what?"

"Not yet. But now I may have to lead the charge. Because it seems as though you're willing to overthrow a government to get on the Princess's good side, while also not being the King."

"...We were going to overthrow it anyway."

Mazigh narrowed his gaze. "I'm counting on everything I know about you, your Majesty, to snap you out of this."

"I am under no spells. I know who I am and what I am doing."

"Tell me you at least see what I am seeing."

"I cannot go around calling her 'Princess,' Mazigh," Max insisted. "Princess of what? As far as anyone knows, she's an American commoner, the daughter of a commoner."

"That's not what I'm talking about and you know it."

"I am going to tell her tomorrow. During the binding ceremony."

"I wasn't really talking about that either, but since you brought it up, it is getting absurd. Do you plan to trample the traditions even further tomorrow? The King is supposed to be with his groomsman the entire day."

"Which will give me an excuse to not break the news in person. No traditions will have to be trampled."

Mazigh knit a skeptical brow. "She should hear it from you."

"She will. In a letter. That will be sent to her. Sealed."

Mazigh seemed satisfied by that.

"It still doesn't explain why you think her 'amaq request has 'merit.'"

"The Ashwari people are going to love her, Mazigh. We may not even need the use of our army."

Mazigh sighed, but he didn't argue. "My King... what you owe me after this is... incalculable."

"I know."

"Do you?"

"I do. I appreciate the thickness with which you are laying it on."

"There was no thickness," Mazigh admitted. "What I said was true. What I said was something you would say. At least, you would have a week ago."

"Not necessarily. The Princess is in a unique position that we may be able to use to our advantage. She handles herself well, does she not?"

Suddenly Mazigh beamed, letting out a smooth laugh the way he always did when they were kids.

It always seemed to him that the throne had aged Emir 100 years. Mazigh hadn't been there to see the young king execute all 50 of his father's so-called "advisors," but he could imagine the sight. There was probably no hesitation. No show of emotion, no flowery address. No warning. The action struck fear in everyone else, even Emir's mother. But no one seemed to understand that the boy had simply been sick with disillusion and mistrust.

Mazigh could always see that Emir was in want of connection, even when he said otherwise. And this half-baked version of him was his most vulnerable yet. Mazigh shook his head as he put both hands on the King's shoulders, his eyes sparkled.

"I'm happy for you, my King. Truly."

Emir cracked a smile. "Don't congratulate me yet."

"You've nothing to worry about, your Majesty."

"She's regretting her decision."

"Only because she thinks she's marrying me."

"Because you're being cruel to her."

"Cruel," Mazigh scoffed. "Realistic, more like."

"Is this what it's like being you? Cleaning up the king's messes?"

"*You told me to be the bad guy!*" said Mazigh in Arabic as the King turned to leave. "And yes, it is!"

"No wonder you are so uncomfortable being me for this long," Emir ribbed him. "The king's vizier appears to be incapable of wrongdoing. Maybe it's time for a career change."

"One day left, your Majesty," Mazigh warned.

* * *

After leaving Mazigh in his private chambers, King Khoury went back to the palace quarters, in search of Gabby.

He got to the Queen's room, dismissing her attendants on the way. They didn't hesitate, though he arrived alone and without his royal guard, closing the door behind him as he entered.

The Queen had arrived with only one suitcase filled with a smattering of sparse belongings. And when Max entered she was currently re-packing that suitcase.

"What are you doing?" he interrupted her.

"I don't know," she confessed, moving back and forth from the massive carved armoire to the open luggage on her oversized canopy bed.

"You do. You are packing."

"I suppose I am."

"Your attendants are more than capable—"

"I'm not calling my attendants in here to pack one suitcase," she calmly cut him off. He ventured another question.

"Where do you plan to go?"

"I don't plan to go anywhere, Mazigh," she sighed on her third trip back to the bed, "because I can't go anywhere. But it makes me feel better."

"You wish to leave."

Max's hurt was palpable. Personal. She stopped mid-trip and lowered her head, letting out a heavy sigh.

"I'm sympathetic to your cause, my Queen. You must believe me," he said.

"Enough," she cut him off. "As if the King doesn't send you in here to play good cop in his absence. Either the King is too lazy or uncaring to speak with me himself, or you are one of the most two-faced men I've ever met. Neither bode well, Mazigh."

Max stood in her path between the armoire and the suitcase.

"It's Max. And sometimes, Queen Asha, there are more than two conclusions to be drawn."

Asha raised an arm in surrender once she realized he wasn't moving until she agreed to listen. "Enlighten me," she said.

"What you proposed is a delicate thing. Manaf has allies, ones that keep the country safe, outside of the U.N.'s jurisdiction."

"And what exactly does Manaf have against the U.N.?"

"An ongoing dispute. Going back to the King's father. They refuse to renounce certain atrocities committed in Manaf by another country which is under their protection."

"Which country?"

"It doesn't matter. Just understand that the allies that keep Manaf protected would not support Ashwari becoming another Arab spring."

"A democracy doesn't necessitate a republic," she retorted.

Max smiled. Which triggered hers.

"What?" she asked.

"I had no idea you had such intellect as well as beauty, my Queen."

"Flattery will get you nowhere with me, Max."

"Touché again. Does anything get by you, my Queen?" he replied.

Gabby smiled. She lived for Max's sudden attempts to be funny. She bit her lip, but it couldn't stop the beaming so she talked instead, moving around him and heading towards the suitcase. This time she was grabbing all her sparse belongings to begin putting them back in their places. It only took a few words from Max to make her lose the will to resist.

"Before I went into nursing, I was planning to major in political science," she explained. "My parents couldn't afford it, so I knew what I had to do to get a free ride. I worked. Hard. Did my extracurriculars. Ran track. Graduated third in my whole class."

"Seems you have been preparing for this role longer than even you realized," he encouraged her.

Gabby rolled her eyes. "I wish I hadn't. According to the king, my job is to hang on his arm whenever he needs it and to bear children. Being educated will only make this job more unbearable than it already is."

When Max was quiet Gabby let out another sad sigh. She scooted the half-empty suitcase behind her and sat on the bed.

"I shouldn't say that in front of you. He's your friend. And you're the second most powerful person in the kingdom."

Max gave her a sleepy grin. "I wouldn't say that."

"I would. Everyone seems to defer to you as if you were the king himself."

Emir tried to backtrack the public interactions he'd had in her presence. He was cutting it close.

"Your unfiltered thoughts are still safe with me, Princess," he said.

"So that you can take it all back to the King?"

"I would never betray your confidence. The more I understand you, the better I can advise the King," he explained.

"So is this what my life will be? You in the middle of the two of us?"

Max gave her an adorable smirk and came and sat beside her on the bed.

The Queen became acutely aware of how they had never been this close. Nothing was keeping her from reaching over and rubbing his back as he said whatever he was going to say. Not because she wanted to touch him, but it just seemed like he needed that.

The truth was, she didn't know if she wanted to touch him, and this wasn't the way to find out. Because if it turned out she did want to, she probably wouldn't have the willpower to stop. And that would be the end of them both.

She glanced toward her window, paranoid someone could see, even though her room sat high in the sky. She got up with a jolt and resumed her re-un-packing.

"I am afraid we have given you the wrong impression of what it means to be Queen. There's only so much that can be explained in a matter of days," Max began. "The king simply spoke of the things he assumed a young woman would want to hear, and the things a king would want to provide his new wife," he said.

Gabby stole glances at his five o'clock shadow that seemed to be evolving from a clean goatee into a beard, which was attractive but taking attention away from his impossibly full lips.

She wanted to ask about it. She found she cared deeply about how Max made decisions of any kind. So mysterious.

"Anything your heart desires would be yours, of course, it's true," he continued, an odd statement to interrupt her thoughts with. "But a certain level of responsibility and leadership is also included."

"Max, you don't have to gas me up," the Queen dismissed.

"Gas you up?"

"Like an air balloon. Inflate my head."

"I would never inflate your head."

"That's a relief."

"You need each other, Princess. It's true that you are the rightful Queen of Ashwari, but you need more than a birthright. You need power. You need an army. The King of Manaf has those things. And perhaps the King is too proud to show it, but he obviously needs you as well. Perhaps more than you need him."

Queen Asha stopped pacing. "Go on..."

"You have much more diplomatic leeway to propose a democracy than the King does. It would've never crossed his mind, in fact. But it would solve several problems. Neither Manaf nor Ashwari needs their allies to grow too powerful. Democracy would neutralize the area. Everyone involved knows that. Only the Ashwari Queen raised in America could propose such a thing."

Gabby flopped back down on the oversized bed, sighing yet again.

Max was right. When he talked that way it seemed like she and the King were a perfect match. This could be beautiful. If she could just stop acting childish and see that. The King had been generous.

"You really think the King needs me?"

"I know that he does."

"He doesn't need Ashwari. And he could have any woman he wants to produce him heirs."

"He doesn't need Ashwari, but he wants it. And he doesn't want those other women. He wants you."

His words sent a shiver through her, oddly. "He told you that?"

Max nodded.

But then she thought of his impatient smile in his private chambers.

"Did he by any chance tell you why?"

"Is it not what we have been speaking about? You are a queen. As beautiful as you are royal. No other woman has been suitable enough for the King before you."

Hadn't Max called her beautiful before? Why hadn't it sent shockwaves through her body then?

"He said that I was old for a princess and that he preferred my sister."

Max let out a rare chuckle, taking her hand. She felt his hand in hers as she watched his smiling face and it nearly killed her.

"I know that the king has been... cryptic with you, but that is merely a defense. It is good politics to act as though you have the upper hand. But I can assure you, Princess, it is you who have it. Once you become his bride, you will come to see that what I am telling you is true."

Max looked down at her as if he would lean in to kiss her. So she became a deer in headlights.

Her voice eeked out, "Do you really think my idea was good? To make Ashwari a democracy?"

"I do."

"Think you could get the King to see things your way?"

"I am confident I can."

"Thank you, Max."

"Of course, my Queen."

"You're really a godsend. I don't think I could do this without you."

Max looked down and put his other hand on top of hers, caressing the top of it with a thumb. An innocent gesture, affectionate. But her sex throbbed intensely with every stroke. She was thankful her legs were crossed. It was her only defense against whatever might happen next.

She was frozen. Her inexperienced virgin body was practically screaming. She didn't dare take her eyes from their hands. She felt found out but there was nothing else she could do. Max seemed to be willfully ignoring her.

"You must continue to be patient with the King," he urged her. "He isn't used to women speaking their own mind. He will learn to appreciate it. As for you, you are a foreigner in a foreign land. You are a princess without a home. Allow yourself time to adjust."

Finally, she pulled herself together, releasing his grasp and making fists of her hands. She avoided the sympathetic void that was his black eyes. A puppy dog, she realized. This tall imposition of a man had the eyes of a puppy dog.

"Where did you learn English?" she suddenly asked.

"Tutors."

"How many languages do you know?"

Max grinned, the signature crinkle along his eyes.

"Why's everything I ask so funny, Max?"

"I don't know."

"Do you know anything?" Gabby found herself asking. Teasing him, of course, but it was the wrong thing to do. Because there was no answer he could give her except his full white smile, which only made her smile, and she couldn't pull her eyes away because it was so damn beautiful.

She saw him lean in but she didn't know what was happening. Only that she felt his lips rest a slow gentle kiss on her forehead.

Loving but not entirely innocent. She didn't know what to make of it. She couldn't explain it away.

Gabby froze, gutted. What the hell was that? She locked eyes with him, looking for more. An explanation, a similar mix of fear and confusion.

But he gave her nothing. Except for a fond examination of her face, as if to memorize it. Then a smirking huff of amusement, as if he were from the future and due back any minute.

"Until tomorrow, young Asha," he said wistfully, reluctantly. In the next second, he was off the bed, a cold weightless absence left in his wake.

It was a sliver of a difference in his voice and the most emotion he'd shown her to date.

He was forlorn. He was saying goodbye. And it frightened her. If she had any inclination that Max was sorry to see her be married tomorrow, she wasn't sure she could do this.

Max was halfway across the room when she snapped out of her trance.

"Will I be able to see you?" she asked.

"I will be at the king's side for most of the evening," he answered in his way that was technically right but conveyed something else entirely.

"So I guess... this is the last time...you and I—"

Max stopped, turning slightly. "Naturally the Queen will not need the King's vizier once she is married. A queen relies on her maidservants."

The emotion had left his voice as quickly as it came.

"Why would the King allow something so unorthodox? Spending so much time with the King's vizier?" she prodded him as she vaulted off the bed.

"Your circumstances are unique, my Queen."

Max continued walking until he was at her door, about to open it. Gabby stopped. "So this is goodbye then."

His eyes found the floor, his hand on the knob. "You mustn't think of it that way," he said.

"How can I not? You're the only friend I have here and I'm about to lose you."

"You can never lose me, my Queen," he said with confidence.

The Queen fumed. What was this? What could that even mean?

"Perhaps I'll have you sent away," Queen Asha proposed.

Max felt a shock through his heart that was part remorse and part intrigue.

He was torturing the girl. She was developing real feelings for Max. Feelings that were going to cause her to say or do something foolish. Reckless. Something that could haunt him for the rest of his life.

He couldn't hold it against her and yet he would. Because he was possessive and sick and growing more irrational by the day.

Would she be saying such things if she knew he was the King? He was essentially growing jealous of himself.

So why couldn't he stop? He turned to face her.

"Why would you send me away, my Queen?"

"You don't think I notice my attendants whispering, each time you come to see me? 'Unorthodox' seems a kind word. How will it be after I am married to the King himself?"

"The King's vizier will not be left alone with the Queen, it's true—"

"So, no more of my unfiltered thoughts."

Max thought of an appropriate answer. "I see no need. You don't need my help anymore, my Queen."

"No, I suppose I don't."

Max turned again to leave, slowly. Confident enough to yield a smirk she couldn't see.

The wedding day couldn't come soon enough. She would be angry, but only for a moment.

In her mind, she was marrying a man she didn't love, who didn't seem to love her. But she wouldn't betray her word. She'd have him sent away before she would.

She was going to see this thing through. She had feelings for him, but she also had resolve, which gave him shivers everywhere.

Max opened her door, half turning his head towards her. "If I have shown impropriety, Princess—"

"Please leave."

Max slowly nodded, keeping composed. "As you wish."

12

Chapter 12

My Lovely Princess Asha:

As I am writing this, I am looking out across the sunrise, and to the north tower, where you will spend your last evening alone.

It is now less than one day until I get to claim you as my wife, my Queen, my prized treasure. You are likely awake now, your attendants dressing you for the occasion of the benediction of the matriarchs.

On days like these, my heart aches more than usual that my mother was not here long enough to bless you with her sweet spirit and limitless stories of the homeland which the two of you share, the homeland which you now hold dear.

My vizier tells me that you have doubts about my affection for you. So allow me to reassure you. You and I have an unspeakable connection, one that has only grown impossibly strong since the day that we met.

Since I learned of your existence, you have been the first thing I think about when I wake, the last thought as I drift to sleep, and the only lasting memory from my dreams. I adore you, my Queen. And I *am devoted to your every happiness.*

Which is why I am reluctant to reveal to you the subsequent thing I have to tell you, though our last moments yesterday give me confidence that this will be more of a relief than a disappointment.

I'm afraid, young Asha, that the truth is I have been deceiving you, even more than you once believed.

The King that has vexed you by bringing you here under false pretenses, who so flippantly alters your circumstance, is not the man whom you have been presented to. Nor is the king's vizier the harmless proxy who bravely advocates for you. Rather, these two men are not separate, but the same.

The king's vizier, Mazigh, who you have known as King Khoury, has only been pretending to be me. While the King has been parading himself as the king's advisor, Max, who is a creation of my own mind.

What began as an extra measure of caution while we investigate the claim of a princess hiding in America, became the King's momentary escape and diversion.

My most trusted advisor has reluctantly aided me in this ruse and has chastised me the entire way through it. He has cautioned me against starting this relationship with deception.

So then, allow me to begin again with you, starting with our first day as husband and wife, King and Queen.

I will speak only for myself when I tell you that I am sad to see Max go, as I relied on him and his ability to charm you and seemingly do no wrong. I will miss the way the Queen trusted him, laughed, and joked with him, and I understand that to continue with the ruse meant forfeiting the rapport that I so effortlessly built. I relinquish it in hopes it will one day return.

In the meantime, I understand that referring to me by my righteous title might be an adjustment. Perhaps once we are united as husband and wife, I will allow you to refer to me as Max in private, if it will make you feel more comfortable. Under the condition that I can keep referring to you as 'my Queen.' Haha!

"*You're an idiot,*" Emir scoffed to himself in Arabic as he balled up another version of his letter and tossed it carelessly to the ground.

He wasn't going to see the Queen again until tomorrow, underneath the wedding canopy, and he hadn't felt such anxiety since his coronation.

He was unsure of himself and irritable. Wanting so much for the Queen to love him had taken his confidence, his patience, and his sleep the night before.

He was an idiot to let it go so long. A selfish idiot with clearly no better outlets. The letter seemed like a good idea yesterday, but it wasn't. It was simply the least of two terrible ideas.

Suddenly there was a knock on the door, and then the sound of his royal guard entering.

He may have been the King, but he was merely Manaf's highest-ranking servant. It's not as though anyone else could handle the task of marrying the Queen. His right to privacy was practically nil.

"My king, your dressers are here."

"I'm aware."

"And your groomsmen are downstairs."

"Let them wait."

Mazigh pushed past the King's guard and walked through the door, sharply dressed in a white Nehru jacket and scarf. He dismissed the rest of the King's attendants and closed the door behind them. Still, he kept his language discreet.

"Just pick the next to last draft, my King. It's usually the one you choose."

"It has to be perfect."

"No one can eat until you arrive."

"No one will starve."

"Shall I write it?"

The King looked up from his pen and paper. "Is it not you complaining that she should hear it from me and no one else?"

Mazigh sighed. "Then let me choose the letter, my King. Go. You're late."

The King reluctantly rose from his writing desk, the tension of the day both urging him to keep the reveal from coming and hasten it to the bedding ceremony.

"Make me look good, Mazigh."

"Don't I always?"

* * *

Meanwhile, Queen Asha was potentially having the worst day of her life.

She hardly slept. She kept having dreams that she'd married a king without a face.

Or at least, she couldn't confirm whether or not he had a face. He seemed incapable of looking at her. She was constantly walking up to him, touching his shoulder, only to have him walk away or further turn away from her.

When her attendants came to retrieve her at sunrise she wasn't asleep. Even though she felt as though she could keel over, misery kept her restless. A hard pit of fear had formed in her stomach and no mental exercise could remove it.

She thought she could reason her way through it, but now the day was here. And her reality stark.

Turns out duty meant almost nothing to her. Not compared to love.

She wished now that they never met. The man that she relied on to help her was now the man making it impossible to go through with this.

She tortured herself going back through her catalog of memories with Max, looking for signs she might have missed. Signs where his devotion to the King and his future Queen could've somehow been interpreted as... more. And yet she had to just stop.

Her attendants seemed more and more surprised at her increasingly somber mood as they bathed and dressed her. Each time they greeted her with a smile, that smile inevitably waned. Gabby had to assume that the look on her face was simply horrifying.

She was slowly finding out that she simply didn't have it in her to feign the excitement and joy that may as well have been in another universe. She only seemed to be able to ask herself the same question over and over as they washed and brushed her hair into a smooth, shiny cascade: *what am I doing?*

Even Zara seemed too intimidated to openly address the situation.

"The Queen usually says a few words before the meeting of the matriarchs. If the Queen Mother cannot be present," she coached her on the way downstairs.

"How long ago did the Queen Mother pass away?"

"Not yet three years ago, your Majesty."

"Do you know how the Queen Mother died?"

"A rare heart defect, I believe, my Queen. May I ask... are you alright?"

Gabby may have stopped midway down the steps, but she

couldn't stop the tears from flowing. Her servants crowded around her, hastily trying to preserve her dark makeup.

She nearly confessed her most acute fears to her attendant, but she suddenly became paranoid that she would simply be deemed as crazy. Every woman here was obviously jealous for the powerful King's affection. Maybe she really was crazy.

"I miss my family terribly today," Gabby sobbed instead, not entirely a lie.

Zara looked empathetic. "I'm sure once you are coronated, the King would be happy to oblige whatever arrangements the Queen would want."

Inadvertently, Gabby had stumbled upon a silver lining. Because Zara was actually right.

The Queen nodded as she straightened herself, wiping her face, feeling strengthened.

She was marrying the wrong man. The day had made that clear. But all was not lost.

She would have power, just as Max said. Power to make her every dream come true. To bring her old life here if she wanted. Maybe she could persuade them all to stay for good if she were a Queen. Maybe her brother would settle down in a place like this, where the women were uncommonly beautiful. Perhaps motherhood would comfort her, as it had comforted Zara's mother.

You can think of him on the wedding night, she tried to console herself. No doubt it would get her through one night. But what about the rest?

Queen Asha was dressed in a beautiful beaded white and gold dress and a gold sash and a bare midriff. Her bangles were stacked from her wrists to her elbows and she was escorted to a vast ballroom covered in ancient patterns of gold and red and purple damask.

Once inside, Gabby managed a few sincere words, much to her own surprise. She let Zara translate between each sentence: "Thank you all for coming. I look forward to being your Queen. I'm very new, so I am relying on all of you for your wisdom. My wish is that we would grow to trust each other and that I will make Manaf proud as Queen."

The elder women nodded graciously. After a beat of silence, she was seated with the rest of her attendants on a mound of pillows, while the older women launched into ceremonial songs she could only understand through context. Zara filled in the rest with her intermittent whispers.

No one suspected or minded the Queen's show of emotion as the ceremony dragged on. She was deliriously tired, had no idea what was being said, and soberly had to face how foreign and alone she truly felt.

She was put through a ceremony of baptism, a mixture of oils and water put through her hair that seemed to drip between her eyes incessantly, no matter how much she toweled off. Her arms and neck were weighted down with the most gold jewelry she'd ever seen in her life, let alone wore. Her attendants helped with the meticulous task of applying mosaics of henna across her wrists and fingers. Their many hands made relatively quick work of it, and not even the trace presence of fragrant oils could get it to smudge.

Her thoughts drifted to Max and whatever he was doing right now. Usually, that helped, but she only felt a tinge of excitement shrouded in bitterness.

She shouldn't have said what she said yesterday. Threatening to send him away. It was something she barely had the power to do, and the thought of manipulating the King to get such a thing accomplished was a bad omen of the kind of queen she never wanted to be.

She only thought she meant it. She had a strange need to wound him at the time. But she was simply not as strong as all that. She could never send him away. The very thought of it made her want to jump off a ledge.

However sick it was, she needed him close. She would never be allowed to say that, but he must know it. She'd likely spend her life sniping at him whenever he was near, asking if he was going to be wherever she and the King were, and then showing disdain.

What if she'd never been brave, or drawn to her duty? What if it was all his doing? What if he was the only good thing about coming to Manaf? This whole time?

"I must say, my Queen, you are a great beauty."

"You are too kind."

"The King is fortunate to have found you. He has been under tremendous pressure to marry since he was a young man."

"I get the impression that the King has had his fair share of suitors."

"Indeed. He and the King's vizier gained quite a reputation when they came of age."

The King's vizier? Has a reputation?

"Really?"

"Oh yes. Mazigh was a bit of a bad influence. But in a good way. The King has always been very dutiful. The Queen Mother insisted he was simply good at hiding his fear of women."

"Well. He's certainly faced that fear head-on."

The women laughed with a tinge of mischief.

"King Khoury is a very private King. For good reason. Very wary to trust. You must be a unique soul indeed to capture his affection."

Asha could only smile. She had no clue what these women could be talking about. But it was the only other insight she'd gotten into the King besides Mazigh's.

"Why is the King's vizier not married?" she wondered. Zara donned a puzzled look that no one else saw.

"Mazigh? Well, I imagine his position is quite demanding. The King trusts him as he trusts himself. The two have been virtually inseparable since boyhood. Though, now that the King is marrying, Mazigh will be freer to follow his own pursuits. This will be quite the adjustment for him."

Gabby suddenly was hit with the sickest shiver yet as a block formed in her stomach.

The two may be inseparable, but she had only been in the same room with them a handful of times. The King regarded her as furniture. And Max... didn't like her to call him by his full name.

Could it be that... such an honor was only reserved for... the King?

Nonsense, she thought, sweating as she shook her head. Max was affectionate towards her. There was a spark.

But then again... she knew very little about romance in general. Perhaps he was simply the gentler of the two?

"You must have many questions, my Queen. About what to expect during the bedding ceremony..."

Perhaps... that kiss on the forehead yesterday was because... the day of keeping up appearances was almost here? Was Gabby taking his place?

The culture was far more strict here. Manaf would certainly not accept a gay king.

Perhaps she wasn't supposed to find out for months. Perhaps there would be no wedding night for her to dread. That wouldn't be so bad.

But it also meant that there would be no Mazigh. Not now or ever.

"The Queen Mother, may she rest, used to worry for her boy king, that he would choose with his mind rather than his heart."

"She should rest easy then, knowing the King did the opposite. Though an Ashwari bride from America would have her beside herself."

"How on Earth did he manage to find her?"

"Would it be possible to get some air?" the Queen turned to Zara, unaware that they were openly discussing her since they weren't speaking English.

"Of course," Zara said with a nod of her head. She clapped her hands and her entire entourage of ten rose around her.

Gabby sighed. Not quite what she had in mind, but okay.

"*The Queen would like to be excused*," Zara announced in Arabic. The Queen led the way as her attendants trailed her out of the banquet hall doors. She didn't quite know where she was going, but it didn't matter.

The sun was already setting, and she realized the day had been moving faster than she gave it credit for.

She was suddenly panicked. Nearly twelve hours left of freedom.

Fresh paranoia stalked her. If she demanded the truth from the King here and now would he even give it?

Perhaps she could coax the truth out of Max. If she could somehow get a message to him.

She could see the distant landmass that she knew was Ashwari from the palace courtyard. Her destiny. Oddly she still wanted it, even though this new theory was tying her in knots.

There was no home for her to run away to. Max had been right.

She needed the King. And he needed her. But what if it was a match made in hell?

She dropped to her knees, her eyes on Ashwari across the water. She couldn't simply get in a boat and row over there. She wasn't safe there, even if she tried to shave her head and live as an unknown. King Khoury would find her. And he wouldn't be happy when he did.

Power through, Gabby. This is your destiny and there's no turning back.

"My Queen, are you alright?"

Honestly, two out of three is damned good. How could she let something so trivial debilitate her, she thought. She never knew love. And what she thought she felt was laughably incorrect and embarrassing. She needed to stop being a child and come into herself. Into her power.

"Zara, I think I'm having a panic attack."

"What can I do, my Queen?"

Asha shut her eyes tight to stop the spinning but the spots wouldn't disappear.

"Find Mazigh," she gasped. She felt Zara leave her side as she opened her eyes again, trembling. She let a tear fall and slowed her breathing.

You can do this... you can do this...

* * *

"We never thought this day would come!"

"Nor did I."

"You were the youngest to become King in Manafi history and the oldest to marry."

"To many more superlatives."

"*Bisihatek!*" *Here here!* they cheered.

The King was surrounded by his groomsman and his lords in waiting. And of course, Mazigh. The room was filled with cigar smoke.

He was less of a King today and more of a groom. His attendants seemed to relish in the ability to tease him good-naturedly, more than they are ever allowed to on any other day.

Emir too was enjoying this temporary status of equality among his men. No wonder his predecessors enjoyed many more festivities during their reigns. Once he and the Queen were together, he imagined there would be many more parties. Now that he had occasion to have them.

"Your mother very much looked forward to this day."

"May she rest."

"She would weep to know that you found a bride from her homeland."

"The former Queen considered Manaf her home. But I hope wherever she is, she feels honored."

"*Bisihatek!*"

"Did the King's vizier deliver the correspondence I entrusted to him?" Emir cryptically asked.

"It will be delivered into the Queen's hand personally, my King," Mazigh assured him.

"It hasn't yet?"

"I've told them to send word once it is delivered."

The King shifted uncomfortably in his chair. It was like waiting for a report on the damage after dropping a bomb. Butterflies flooded his chest.

"I want someone to report to me on the Queen's reaction."

Awwws were heard around the room, followed by melting laughter. His cabinet all assumed the mushiest. The King further

165

betrayed himself with a slinking smile.

"To the King's newfound romance!"

"To the future Queen!"

"*Bisihatek!*"

"Who knew America could be the place for so many kings to find brides?"

"Both you and King Belkacem have made it harder for us at home!"

"My brother's Ghassani wife is working him to death trying to keep up with Queen Kimberly's latest fashions."

"The Queen of Manaf will not be concerned with such frivolity."

A few of the men gave the commenter a disapproving look, knowing King Khoury's close relationship with Ghassan. Luckily, the King didn't seem to be listening.

There seemed to be something at the door demanding attention, the King noticed. One man went to the door, returned, and brought back another. Then the two returned to inform someone else until the chain reached Mazigh.

King Khoury knew what it must mean, and he was annoyed. No one wanted to bother him, of course, but whatever it was, it was clearly bad enough to warrant Mazigh's attention, which meant it warranted his attention. It wasn't life-threatening, but bad enough that no one was willing to incur his wrath. It had to be about the Queen.

"What is it?" King Khoury finally asked himself.

"I can handle it, your Majesty."

"Mazigh. Just tell me."

"Apparently... the Queen has been... misplaced."

The King's brow rose.

"...Misplaced?"

"She's obviously somewhere on the palace grounds."

"How did she become 'misplaced'?"

"The details are unclear, but her attendants lost sight of her."

"Was she.... running?"

Mazigh remained silent, trying to help the King save face in an uncomfortable room.

But the King couldn't be bothered with what his attendants thought of his colossal fuck-up. This was obviously his fault.

She'd read the letter. And she hated him enough to try and escape.

"What did you put in that letter Mazigh?"

"I put none of my own words in it, my King."

Well. That he did believe. His words were enough to frighten her for good. He sighed.

"This is my fault. I will go after her."

"You heard the King," Mazigh addressed the royal guard.

"Alone."

"My King, at least take your men."

"Am I not safe in my own palace?"

"It could be a trap... my King. Someone could have—"

"Found out? How could they possibly?"

"I don't know. I just don't have a good feeling about it."

"Not even the General would ambush me during a wedding. It is much more likely this is due to the contents of my letter."

"My King," a female voice spoke, "the letter is right here. When I reached the banquet room the Queen and her attendants had been gone for some time. They returned without her."

King Khoury reached out to summon the letter and the young maid came forward with it, placing it in his open hand. The seal remained unbroken.

If it wasn't the content of his letter that caused this, then what was?

"Everyone split up. The more of us there are, the sooner we will find my fianceé."

"What should we do when she is found?"

The King realized then that he might want to leave the search party to everyone else if he was going to maintain his cover.

He didn't care about his silly ruse anymore. But there were better ways of unveiling it that wouldn't involve her humiliation.

"Take her back to her chambers. The ceremony will continue as planned."

Mazigh drew closer as everyone filed out.

"Are you sure everyone here can be trusted?"

"It is not like you to be so paranoid, friend."

"It's unlike you to not be."

"Only seven souls know the Queen's full identity. Based on our last interaction, and the fact that the letter remains unopened, it is likely the Queen has acted upon false assumptions. If by chance, I have fallen victim to yet another treacherous cabinet, no soul will be left alive. If it is you who has betrayed me, no soul will be left alive. I must believe that this is merely the frantic actions of a scared young girl. I will leave you to handle the worst-case scenario."

"To scared young girls," Mazigh sighed. Emir gave him a slap on the shoulder as they parted ways.

"*Bisihatek.*"

* * *

The King was escorted to one of the nearby guest chambers on the ground floor of the palace for the night with a few of his guards. The King's chamber was being prepared for the bedding ceremony.

"Let me know when the Princess has been recovered."

"At once, your Majesty."

Emir sighed. It was going to be another sleepless night. He wasn't worried about the princess. She was safe on the palace grounds and would likely be found within the hour. But he worried about her state of mind.

He slowly walked out to his balcony, the Queen's chamber on the opposite side of his, within view from where he stood in the guest room. His view from his place on the guest patio was like Romeo's view of Juliet. He saw no movement besides the occasional maid, frantically retracing her steps.

"'*Amaq*," he muttered to himself. Perhaps it wasn't the best idea to keep her confined to her chambers once she was found. She might do something even more drastic. He had to admit that he'd made a mess of this. Perhaps he could sneak out past his guard and visit her. Early, before the sun came up.

Nonsense, he should get over himself entirely and join the search. This was all his fault after all.

"Max?" he suddenly heard a small voice from the corner. The shadow of her royal garments swallowed her slight body like a royal growth.

"My Queen," Max replied, stunned yet composed. What were the odds?

"Max," she said again, relieved.

"How did you get in here?" he wondered, charmed. Though he should probably be disturbed.

His royal guard had all been with him. A missing Queen was quite the diversion, but still. An unarmed woman shouldn't be able to make it near the king's quarters undetected. Though the implications were unexpectedly arousing.

"How many are looking for me?"

"Everyone is looking for you," he replied.

"Everyone? Even the King?"

"Even the King," he pretended without hesitation. "He wanted to go after you alone but his vizier advised against it. He felt... responsible. For your emotional state."

"Did he seem worried? Or... angry?"

Max smirked. "He tried to keep on a brave face, but I could tell he was deathly afraid."

The Queen scoffed as she fiddled with her white polished nails. "I've never known you to be over-dramatic, Max."

"Which is why you must know I am telling the truth."

"Was he afraid that all of his carefully laid plans may have come to ruin?" she bitterly assumed.

"He was afraid that someone may have captured you. That all of his stealth was not enough, and that he had somehow followed in the footsteps of his father, trusting the most valuable thing to him to wicked traitors. This is his worst fear, in fact."

Gabby hit the back of her covered head against the terrace wall in defeat. Horror.

Now she was wounding the man. He didn't deserve that. It made her heart hurt and she felt like she was being torn apart.

Max always knew how to explain the King in a way that made her feel. If her theory was right, then that would explain a lot.

Warm tears filled her eyes as she looked up at the night sky.

"Please tell the King that I'm sorry. It was reckless of me. Foolish. Please apologize to my attendants. To the palace."

"If you really want to make amends you will tell the King yourself. Tomorrow. Under the wedding canopy."

Her extravagant jewelry jingled across her body as she shook her head soberly. "I can't."

"Why not?"

"Because I'm afraid. Tremendously," Asha croaked.

"Afraid of what?"

The Queen's throat felt as though it would close permanently and never re-open. She swallowed. The disappointment in Max's voice confused her terribly. Her tears quickly fell and cooled in the desert night wind.

"I'm afraid that I cannot marry the King."

13

Chapter 13

Max was stock still. He felt a lifetime go by in silence.
"Why now? What's changed?"

She emerged from the shadows of the guest room terrace. He barely recognized his Queen, covered in makeup and henna and gold.

"Nothing's changed. I knew what this was going to be. From the moment I saw him..." Asha stopped, the dam threatening to burst.

She meant the King, but she knew in her heart that she was talking about Max. She was in love with him. Whether he could love her or not.

"From the moment I laid eyes on him... I think I knew that I couldn't do it... but I didn't understand what I knew. I didn't feel... I thought I could overcome it like it was nothing. And now... now I feel like I might die." Her explanation came out in a cryptic garble of emotion.

The King somehow imagined that she knew that she was talking about him. Even though she hadn't opened the letter.

"My Queen, I know that we have asked much of you. I

understand you may miss your home and family—"

"It's not that. There is... another," the Queen blurted impatiently as she turned away from him.

Max's heart doubled speed. And yet her vague confession enflamed his insecurities. Her eyes hit the floor.

"Is this... someone you left behind? In the States?"

"It is not."

Max flexed his fist in covert celebration. Was this not the perfect moment to reveal himself?

"My Queen... who is this traitor to the crown?" he asked.

She looked up. "He's not a traitor," she defended. "Nor am I. Not yet."

Not yet?

"I don't understand."

The Queen didn't blink. "Tell me, do you think the King is attracted to me? I demand you tell me the truth."

"The King is enthralled with you."

"You're a liar, Max," Gabby insisted with an atrophied laugh.

"I am not."

The Queen suddenly exploded, brimming with frustration.

"You lie to your Queen! How dare you! How can he trust you? How can I? When you lie to my face?"

Max was unable to speak as Asha whirled around to conceal her tear-stained face. She was so dignified when she was angry.

The King was nauseous with guilt. He was so blinded by his own ruse that he'd refused to see anything past her own mask of composure. He'd been tearing her apart.

He should've kept himself away. If he couldn't manage that, the least he could've done was kept his hands to himself. And his lips.

"Tell me the truth. Does the King admire *any* women?" she

suddenly speared through his guilty musings.

"...Princess. What are you implying?" he firmly asked, a furrow denting his brow.

Queen Asha pressed on in bitterness, though her theory was breaking apart by the second.

"My attendants tell me the King is under pressure to marry. And they're relieved that I am here."

The two stood in a silent standoff. Asha shook her head and threw up her hands in resignation.

"What am I walking into, Max? At least be decent enough to tell me. Am I here just to be a cover? So he can pursue his true appetites in peace and quiet? And acquire my country in the process?"

"Careful, young Asha," Max lowly warned as he moved forward a step, "before your imagination costs you more than just a crown."

Her nipples perked and she lost her breath.

Okay, so she was wrong about her theory— possibly in trouble now— but remained uncomforted. She was still convinced the two of them were hiding something.

The Queen laughed in exasperation at his informal address, more tears falling. "Listen to you. You treat me like a child. All of you do. Can you honestly blame me for assuming the worst? He doesn't touch me, he doesn't look at me, he just... smiles. He is *clearly* exasperated by me in private. And you..."

Her weighty garments rustled as she began to slowly walk towards him. He found himself unable to move or look away as she closed the distance between them. She grabbed the hand at his side and placed it on her wet face. Nestling into it, holding it there with her own. His mouth dried as he watched the young girl woo him.

"*You* touch me. *You* look at me. And you never smile. Except for... when you do. And in private? In private you are... kind. Gentle. Patient. Careful," she cooed, comforted by his touch, the fact that he didn't recoil in response to her. She faced the fear in his eyes.

"And all you've done since the moment we met is lie."

His heart continued to pulsate. He was stunned by her. She knew him, and she knew the truth— and yet, she clearly didn't.

Did she mean... the faked documents? He didn't deny it.

"It was for your protection."

"Another lie."

Max's courage waned. Part of him still didn't want out. From her perspective, she was risking her life at this point and she knew it. It touched him so. He'd never felt so vulnerable as he did with Queen Asha, and yet he also hadn't felt so free.

He retracted the hand she held captive. Her look of shock and hurt caused him to pace, looking out for anyone who could spot them. Fuck. He should've bothered to bring the letter with him. He was going to have to wing this.

"Try to see his dilemma, my Queen," he began, pulling her into the shadows by her hands. He held them close to his chest, pleading for her sympathies.

"The King's father lost his life trusting those closest to him," he reasoned. "Because of this, he tends to keep people at arm's length. For longer than he should, perhaps. But it will not always be that way."

The Queen searched his eyes and seemed to be put at ease at his words, and suddenly he didn't know how to feel.

"I think you're telling the truth now," she replied soberly, embarrassment and guilt nearly drowning out her panic, "and I want to see him the way you seem to. To love him. But I simply...

175

can't."

For a brief irrational moment, his insecurity took over his mind at her words. So that was it? She was done?

He was jealous of himself again, imagining himself as the King in her scenario, not the other man that he pretended to be.

He imagined himself on the other side of the palace, frantically looking for her, while she fought her feelings outside on the king's balcony with his vizier.

And that's when he felt it. A flicker of arousal, alight in the very center of him, radiating out like a sun, and he found it very peculiar. Dangerous to entertain. Did the thought of her infidelity turn him on?

Impossible. It made no sense. Yesterday it was her fidelity that aroused him. How could it now be her confession of weakness?

And that's when he suddenly realized that he was an animal. Worse, a man. That was bored with success.

Because he knew then the real reason that he hadn't confessed until now. It wasn't for her benefit, how could it be? The reality was his lust for the virgin Queen outweighed his affection. And he was about to drag this charade out to the very last second.

"The King has shown you respect and trust, these four days you've been out of his sight," he ventured. "Was he wrong to do that?"

Asha stepped away, looking insulted as she removed her hands from his. "So that's how it will be?" she coldly asked. "You pretend to be innocent? Don't tell me you didn't know what you were doing. You knew my inexperience. You would have me believe I am in this alone?"

"You are not," was his low confession. Max walked toward her slowly, reveling in her confused, fearful demeanor. The Queen didn't flinch but was unwilling to meet his eyes. He was close enough that he could feel her tremble.

"But I would never betray my King in such a way," he added.

For an impossible moment, everything stilled. She still refused to look at him, though he was looking softly at her gorgeously dressed shape, his body begging her to make him into a liar.

"But I would?" she filled in, bitterly.

To his dismay, her manner became rigid. Furious.

"Gabby—"

"How dare you turn this back on me!" she scowled in a whisper, her breath coming out in heaves of quiet outrage. "I could do this with anyone but you by his side. Anyone!" she cried.

He grabbed at her arm, trying to subdue her without drawing much attention, but she easily broke free. She turned to run away from him, slipping on the hem of her dress and stumbling as she broke into a run.

Ugh. What a piece of shit he was, he thought, paralyzed. Asha left the patio doors open behind her, her sobs echoing along the walls inside. He breathed a curse to himself.

"Princess, wait..." Max dashed after her, scanning the room for signs of her once he was back inside.

Odd. Had she run out that fast? He searched the room a moment before he was satisfied she was no longer there.

He headed down the hallway to the atrium, where there was a trail of discarded gold jewelry going down the hall. He followed it until it stopped in front of the indoor courtyard, surrounding an indoor pool. She must've cut through.

Damn, she was fast. He thought of that picture of her standing in her track shorts, holding up the winning medal.

"Gabby?" he called out.

"Just leave me alone, Max," he heard her voice to the left of him. She was close. Probably didn't realize the circle she was running in.

He cut her off in front of the trickling middle fountain twinkling under the moonlight. This time he grabbed her by the arm and whirled her around, drawing her close, so close that she tightened with apprehension mixed with longing. Her breath labored from trying to escape him.

"Let me go..." she weakly protested.

"No," he panted.

"No? I thought you said... you could never betray the King," she dared him, accusatory in her tone. He imagined the respect she had for him slowly draining away.

I am the king... the confession was on his tongue. Ready to put her at ease.

But he didn't want her ease. At least, the hardening length between his legs didn't.

"Max, what are you doing," she whispered in fear, the consequences of her confrontation too real now. She was breathing so hard now, the way she did in his fantasies. Or was that his breath? He was drunk with desire.

"This isn't like you," she whispered through her heaving breaths. "If someone sees us I'm dead. You know that."

It was a valid fear, just not for the reasons she thought. The only thing in danger of death tonight was her virtue.

He imagined there was no King in Manaf's history who managed to go the full two weeks of the wedding ritual without de-flowering the Queen before the wedding night.

But three days was probably a record.

"I would never, ever let anything happen to you," he swore.

"How could you stop it from the grave?" she sobbed, wriggling in his grasp. "Please leave me alone. If something happened to you because of me... I won't let you lose your life over me."

The King was overwhelmed by her words, guilt warring with his arousal. He held onto her firmly until she tired, the two of them winded.

"I already have lost it, my Queen. Because of you," he confessed. "The moment I laid eyes on you. From the moment we met, my life as I knew it was over."

She stopped, shivering. Her eyes widened at his audacious confession. Of all the things he could've said, she wasn't expecting that.

"I don't understand," her expression frozen.

But she did. She just didn't want to. She didn't want to comprehend Max feeling this way from their first meeting. It was too much.

Her mind went back to the awkward introduction in the old living room of her old life. The first time he'd probably laid eyes on her she'd burst out of a steamy bathroom in that ugly mauve towel. She mentally cringed.

"I love you, Princess Asha Gabrielle Otieno," he shocked her again.

Holy crap.

"Max..." she gasped, suddenly infused with understanding. Before she could go on, Max grabbed her face in his hands and began to kiss her.

Could it be that she had always known? Is that what made the King's presence seem so paltry in comparison?

She was still grasping for context as she resisted him with her stiff body, fighting herself more than him as he gave her the first real kiss of her life. Her lips were tight and unyielding at first as if to reject him. She breathed through her nostrils frantically.

He broke away from her in the frantic quiet. He clasped both her hands in one of his and pulled her to a pitch-black corner of the courtyard. He kept his back to the palace wall as he situated her before him.

"Shhh... it's okay," he panted, trying to catch his own breath as they held onto each other in the dark. He could only make out her silhouette as his fingers felt her chin. His thumb trailed her lower lip until he felt it loosen from its pucker, finally going slack, her breath hitting his hand in gusts.

Slowly he leaned in until their lips were stacked, barely touching. His fingertips ventured softly down her throat and she moaned, as if she were desperate to give in and complete the circuit. But she simply couldn't.

The confession came to him again: *I am the king.*

No way, his dick said. Princess Asha was letting the king's vizier feel her up outside the courtyard and he'd never been so turned on his life.

Besides, it wouldn't make a lick of sense right now. Once it clicks, there'll be no more kissing. There'll be questions. Probably yelling, knowing the Princess. And his dick didn't want any of that.

Finally, his full mouth clasped hers, slowly, savoring every sweet nanosecond of reciprocation.

"Stop," she managed to eek out between tongue touches. He vowed to never forget her gasps of terrified pleasure as he drank and drank from her lips, as he tasted up and down her jawline, salty from wet tears. The smooth skin of her neck, her muffled pleas for him to stop, the pungent scent of her betrayal.

He'd never done something so wrong, and he wished he could fool her forever. He had less than twelve hours left before this was utterly ruined, and this is what he wanted to be doing during it.

Far off voices in the distance snapped them out of their reverie. They froze, trying to decipher the direction the disembodied voices were walking in.

When the voices dimmed again, they eyed each other as much as they could in the darkness.

"I have an idea," Max breathed. "Come with me."

"We can't do this, Mazigh."

The King bristled. It wasn't his name.

This was a dangerous game. One wrong word, one unbecoming gesture from her could bring it all crashing down. What if her innocence was all an act? What if she was one of those "everything but" virgins?

The King in him wanted to know now, but he was being unfair. Hadn't she done well enough? Must he tempt the fairytale any further?

"Don't call me that," he whispered, taking her hand.

"We can't do this, Max," she corrected, her mind barely hanging on to the exhilaration of what just happened, arousal slick and throbbing between her legs with every step she now took. It felt so good that it had to be completely right or completely wrong.

Why hadn't anyone told her what it was like for a man to kiss you? To have his hands all over you?

The king's vizier had been the one to awaken her. How could she marry the King tomorrow without Max giving her the strength?

Suddenly, in the dark, she found her resolve.

She would let Max make love to her. Just this once. Then she would have him sent away.

And imagine this night, every night, for the rest of her life. Perhaps she could conceive his child and raise it.

A thunderous sword thrust straight through her heart and she tried not to cry. That would give her the courage to possibly never know love like this again. That would give her the courage to possibly know a portion of it through someone else.

They wormed their way across the courtyard like thieves, the Princess always one step behind him. Both their parties would be looking for them so they had to be careful.

While the Queen was out of her head with anxiety and conflicting emotions, the King was simply worried someone would run into them and call him "your Majesty."

He led her away from the palace to a sandy hill that led to a small beach. He was relieved to find the small rowboat still tied to the tiny dock at the bottom.

"I can't swim," she warned him.

"I will teach you," he said. "Another time. But for now, I need you to keep quiet, and trust me."

When they got to the boat, Max had her lay down in the bottom. He threw a burlap tarp over her and all she heard was the sound of the water and the monotonous strokes of the paddles. All she could see was the moon glow through the holes of the fabric. Her mind was ringing with one singular question repeating: *what are we doing??*

Finally, she felt them come to a stop.

"The coast is clear. You can come out," Max bellowed at full voice, lifting the tarp off of her.

The Queen looked around to see that Manaf was essentially gone. They looked to be on the edge of the world.

He made his way out of the boat and reached for her hand once he was standing atop the dock. She took his hand and looked up to see the biggest, brightest moon she'd ever seen. Nothing was heard besides the sound of the light blue water turned black by the darkness.

"Shouldn't we let someone know that I'm safe?" Gabby suddenly wondered.

"l will," Max promised. "Don't worry."

They were surrounded by water. From the light of the moon, she could barely make out the palace that was a ways off in the distance. In front of her was a short dock that led to the mouth of a cave.

In the moonlight, she saw him bend near the entrance and heard the opening of a creaky metal box. Suddenly there was a hum and the cave was lined with soft canned lights along its walls. Max took her hand.

"No one will disturb us here," he assured her.

The cave appeared millennia old. It was naturally hewn along the sides, presumably by men long forgotten. The cave twisted a bit until it finally opened to a large room lined with beautiful brick masonry. A staircase led to a balcony and another unseen room. Underneath it was a loft-style set up with a bed. A grotto filled with clear blue water sat directly in the center, with a large chandelier hanging above it.

"This is... breathtaking," she said, her hand still in his as he led her.

"It is," he agreed as he led her by the hand to the center of it.

"This is my fortress of solitude. Whenever I feel the need to get away for a while, but my duties keep me from straying too far from the palace." He turned and hooked the other arm around her waist.

"Is this where the magic happens?" Gabby joked, even though her nerves were frayed by his touch.

"The magic?"

"You know. Where you bring the ladies," she smiled.

"I have never shown any woman this place. No one except you," he replied, the intense look in his eye now completely visible. Was he looking at her that way in the courtyard? Gabby gulped.

"Then why is there such a big bed in here?" she softly challenged.

"I like big beds," he shrugged.

Queen Asha laughed. Max smiled. He cupped her face in his big hand and the look in his eye sobered her. She felt like a child and she suddenly wondered if she was ready to marry any man.

But there was no time for second-guessing. She was getting married in the morning. It was now or never.

She didn't think of Max as the kind of man who would let her go through with this, and it should have changed her opinion of him. But she couldn't afford to do anything but enjoy this moment.

She got down to brass tax.

"We do this once," she began shakily, "and never speak of it again."

"Only once, my Queen?" he replied in his low rumble, daring to fluster her. But she didn't return his tease.

Her cheeks grew hot. "I'm afraid I won't have the slightest clue what to do."

The King was enamored. "You seemed to know very well what to do in the courtyard."

"I wasn't doing anything," she confessed. "Except maybe holding on for dear life."

Max chuckled a bit as he kissed her cheek, which became a nip to her earlobe.

"That's all I ask," he whispered.

Gabby complied, slinking her arms around his neck as he continued to stimulate her virgin skin with the silk of his mouth and the weight of his arm slinked around her waist. She relied on him to hold her as she started to let herself unravel in his arms.

Queen Asha breathed with anxiety, willing her eyes open as his lips finally returned to hers. She broke away, breathless. Max cursed inwardly.

He brought her here so that she could fully relax. But he was being selfish. He couldn't expect the Princess to plow through her conscience for him at the pace that he expected. She eyed the elaborate chandelier above them as she broached the obvious subject.

"The King... will know, will he not?" she asked in a small voice. "Or at least... suspect?"

"The King is blind with affection for you," he quickly panted, nuzzling her lips with his. "You can do no wrong in his eyes," he said with a pillowy kiss.

At that, she suddenly stopped.

Maybe it was because Max was talking to her in a way he never had before. Or rather, saying the same things he always does while being a completely different person to her.

But she had that same odd feeling that he was telling the truth, even though it seemed like a lie. And for a split second, she had a thought she'd never had before.

It all made perfect sense... if Max was really the king.

"I sometimes pretended to be him on diplomatic errands..."

The thought arrested her and her body seized with so much hope that she was too afraid to do anything but look back at his eyes.

He returned her gaze but seemed not to see the question in hers, focused instead on savoring the sight of her lips before they reconnected. She watched his eyes close rapturously.

She felt his lips on her neck again and it was so glorious, that her questions started to fade.

Broaching the subject became an incredibly foolish prospect. What if she was wrong? Her questions would only sting him, sever this delicate bliss she may not ever have again. And if she was right...

"An hour of anonymity was sometimes all the King desired."

She shivered as her hope became unbearable, mingling with the passion infecting her and her nails dug into his flesh. She smeared her kisses all over his mouth, the scrape of his scruffy shadow stinging her delicate skin. She searched for his tongue in reckless abandon. When she found it, he hoisted her on his hips, carrying her over to his bed and gently laying her down.

As Max hovered over her, trailing his hands down her body as he kissed her relentlessly, she resolved to be satisfied no matter what her reality revealed itself to be tomorrow. In her heart, he was her King. And that was all that mattered.

14

Chapter 14

"**M**ax?"

He was gingerly removing her gold sash, devising a strategy for what else to take off, and what to do about it, how far they should go. Her small voice stopped him abruptly. He straightened up to look directly into her heavy-lidded eyes, breathless.

"Can you... show me? How to please the King?"

He tried not to look stunned by her request as he gave her a drunken nod. He stroked her face and then sat up on the bed.

"Have you ever seen a man?" he bluntly asked. There was the Max she recognized.

"...Not in person," she cryptically admitted. He stifled a smile as she rolled over and propped herself up on one elbow, grinning. She was obviously expecting a show. She bit her lip.

Max undid the front ties on his tunic, revealing his smooth chest only slightly before bringing the garment up over his head, his top half entirely exposed. She took in the sight of his beautiful build, his dark smooth shoulders, his sturdy arms.

His erection was now uncovered by the drape of his top,

pronounced proudly through his fine linen trousers. He got up on his knees to pull them down and she could only imagine the look on her face as Max revealed to her his naked body.

The girthy protrusion she felt earlier that night through her dress, the pressure lining up perfectly with her sex, was exactly what she'd suspected it was. She felt dread in the pit of her stomach as she confronted her distantly pondered suspicions head-on.

Max was hung. Like a horse.

She couldn't take her eyes off of it, bouncing about as if to taunt her. If Max was worried for her she couldn't tell, but he seemed to know what she was thinking.

He took his time laying down to shed his trousers the rest of the way, laying on his back with an arm underneath his head.

As he lay there completely naked, bare in front of his fully clothed Queen, his dick stretched toward the chandelier, he fought the urge to caress his thighs and stroke himself, basking in the shy, awestruck watchfulness of the Queen.

"Come here," he finally said.

The mysterious drip-drip of water from somewhere in the ancient catacombs was the only sound as it hit the grotto below, its shimmering glow reflecting all over the bed and Max's naked form. Asha inched to the head of the bed on her hands and knees. She knelt on the bed and removed the pins from her hair, shaking it in relief.

Max smiled as the Queen disheveled herself and began to undress right next to him, facing him, unbuttoning the bodice of her top and slinking it down one shoulder and then the other. She wore no bra, and presumably no underwear. He licked his lips.

She raised up from the resting position on her knees to bring the dress down further, but Max stopped her, reaching out to her wordlessly with a look in his eye, as though she were a statue come to life. He grabbed her arm, urging her closer until she straddled his long torso, his erection against her back...

He sat up from his laying position just enough to be eye level to her chest, the folds of her gown bunched up at her waist, now exposing her smooth legs. He let his hand disappear underneath the royal fabric, searching for her wet warmth as he took in the sight of her pert breasts, now unleashed and taking up his whole line of sight from where his head lay, like some majestic mountainside.

Her nipples were impossibly dark and taut. His neck stretched like a turtle as he tried to taste one without having to remove his hand from between her thighs. Or his head from its place near her cleavage, where she seemed to loom over him like a giant, the way she did in his subconscious. He rested his cheek on the skin of her bosom as he looked up at her like a beggar who'd been taken in by a benevolent angel. She held his head with one of her hands like a baby's.

She could only look down at him with a blank stare, mouth agape as the slow ministrations of his fingers began to build a frenzy of sensation between her legs. His mouth too began to slack as the Queen began to roll gently across his hand, now slick with her own arousal.

He teased a nipple with the tip of his tongue and the Queen let out a whimper that was more frustration than pleasure. His hand too began to sway rhythmically underneath the luxurious tent of her wrinkled gown. He let out one groan after another as she saturated his fingers and her binding ceremony gown with her own juices. He wanted it ruined. He rubbed and groaned until she was crying out in choked sobs.

"Come for me, my Queen," he begged. Just like her fantasy. Her heart burned.

"Oh my God," she gasped. Her neck rolled in surrender as the biggest orgasm of her life worked its way up and out of her body. She clasped his shoulder with one hand as her cries bounced off the walls of the cave and spasmed her until she was folded over and shaking.

Max let her collapse on top of him, orgasm still stiffening the muscles in her legs as his length nudged at her slippery sex from behind. Her tightness was already torturing his sensitive tip as she lapped against it. Max winced.

As ready as she was, she was still a virgin. And the way he felt right now, he didn't have the patience to go easy. He could get away with a lot being the King, but if the Queen couldn't even walk tomorrow, he'd feel nothing but shame.

He laid down and hoisted her up a bit, lining up her sex with his. Though her limbs moved like a rag doll's, he felt her knees engage, helping with the task.

His dick felt like it was pushing through a wall. He waited for her body to open up and accept him, but it stayed rigid. He pushed back against that fleshy wall a bit and her legs shook. *Fuck.* He should really save all this for tomorrow night.

Suddenly he felt her bear down with a groan and he abruptly inched his way in. His fingers fanned out in shock, but the inching stopped as though she could go no further.

The majority of his cock was still waiting to find shelter but there was none. He looked up at her face where her eyes were tightly shut.

"I'm hurting you," he deduced. She quickly nodded.

"Then we should stop"

"No," she whimpered.

"Gabby, I'm fine."

"No!" she said, grabbing between her legs for his length with determination. She forced him out and started again and again, causing him to moan and groan. She replied with her own, her channel getting slicker but no more flexible.

"Gabby enough," he winced. Her inexperience was stark. Guilt rose in his throat.

"This is our only chance," she breathed. "I won't risk our lives again after tonight. I can't."

"But there's no need to rush," he groaned with a kiss to her lips.

"How can you say that? You have to take my virginity, Max."

"Why, my Queen," he smiled shyly. Her oblivion only made this covert plot of hers seem more innocent.

Gabby didn't have to hide it anymore. She smiled back before she kissed him. Hard.

"Because it's yours. Not his," she whispered into his mouth.

Max narrowed his eyes to look at her. He raised a hand to her face, spreading a thumb across her bottom lip. He eyed her with possession and her heartbeat doubled.

"You would still like to know how to please the King?"

She nodded.

"You will say that to him."

"It will be a lie."

"You will say it," he gruffly demanded. The Queen lowered her gaze.

"If that's what you want," she lowly conceded.

"It is," he insisted. "Now tell the King. You belong to him."

Gabby rolled her eyes. "My pussy is yours for the taking, o King," she repeated sarcastically.

Max didn't take it that way. His right arm left her waist and went between her legs. He held her by the hip with just his left hand.

"Say it like I told you."

"It's yours, not his," she practiced as he rubbed her still sensitive clit. His fingers found her lingering wetness and followed the trail up and inside her.

The intrusion didn't feel like much of anything to her. It felt like an exam. A second digit entered her. My word! She looked down at the hand that was dominating her. This was the type of Queen coaching she'd been missing.

"Again."

"It's yours, not his," she moaned as a third finger made its way in. His movements became gruff until they created a strange pressure with every thrust, one that seemed to get more pleasurable the more it aroused her.

"Fuck," she let slip with a curious tone.

"I didn't tell you to stop," he said.

"It's yours, not his."

"It's mine?" he asked, his pumping becoming forceful.

"It's yours, not his. *Ah!*" she gasped.

"This is what you are asking for," he said, placing his entire drenched hand inside, stretching her as his thumb circled her clit. "If you want me to take your virginity tonight. Do you want me inside you right now?"

"Yes."

"Why?"

"Because," she gasped "… I want you to impregnate me."

Stunned, Max quickly grabbed her by the waist and impaled her with the tip of his cock. His thrusts were quick and shallow, but Gabby was still holding on for dear life, as she promised she would.

Her cries emptied next to his ear, in the pillow on which he laid his head. His arms were burning as he held her high above his length, careful not to go too far past her limit, which was morphing by the second.

"You would let the king's vizier impregnate the Queen?" he salaciously asked.

"No one would ever find out," she turned to his ear and said, wincing.

Sweat beaded his forehead and his biceps gave out. He let Gabby go and she continued her slow bounces on the tip of his cock. Better than when they started, but not nearly enough.

He put her down and let her support herself with her knees and her new position forced him out. He found her wetness again with his hand, massaging her until he had enough wetness to coat himself with. He began to stroke.

Gabby held still, hovering above his length, awaiting the return of his fisted hand across her clit with every stroke.

"You would let the King put a bastard on the throne?"

"It could be a girl," she cooed.

His balls tightened. Jeez. He really did have the turn-ons of a King.

"You will lay with the King tomorrow night?"

"Yes," she vowed. He licked her top lip.

"And you will think of me?"

"Oh God, yes," she moaned, feeling his tightening grip on her ass. He held her steady right above him, his breath hot on her ear. The steady stroking movement of his powerful arm made the bed almost vibrate.

"Do you want my cum?" he prodded her in a whisper, like a desperate teenager. Her body shuddered.

"I need it, Mazigh," she gasped.

He was so far gone that her saying Mazigh's name was now the hottest fucking thing she could've possibly done. He stroked and stroked and did his best to empty his load into her as he let go and held her by the waist, inserting himself inside, his cock twitching with every release.

He supposed there was some distant chance she could actually get pregnant that way, he thought, as he let out groan after groan, but it hardly mattered. He intended to try again the next night, and the one after, indefinitely. He let her words have their way with his contorted body as orgasm surged through him.

Finally, his right mind could return to him as he pulled out and she relaxed on top of him. Instantly his sperm spilled back out of her.

"Am I still a virgin?" she asked.

"Perhaps. If you still have to ask, my Queen," he panted with his eyes closed.

"Then we'll have to try again."

"I've never seen you so persistent, young Asha."

"It's one of my best qualities," she boasted as she raised up with a smile, giving him a lingering kiss. "I like it when you call me that, Max."

He smiled. "Even more than 'my Queen'?"

"...No," she admitted. He caressed her back as he chuckled. They lay in the quiet, reasonably satisfied, for the first time since they met.

Maybe now's the time, he thought.

"Gabby..."

She raised up to look at him, stars in her eyes.

More than stars. An intuition that wasn't there before.

Not just intuition, knowing.

She already knew.

194

Why hadn't she confronted him? Was she humoring him? Pitying him?

Did she really have a choice? All he'd had to do was confirm it. And yet, time and again he'd denied himself the opportunity.

And he was about to do it again. The knowing in her face shrunk him to the size of an ant.

"...Would you... like a swimming lesson?" Max said instead.

The Princess scoffed. "Now?"

"We should tackle as many firsts together as we can. My Queen," he said.

Emotion overcame her as she giggled. She nodded.

"Very well, Mazigh."

"Call me Max, my Queen."

Asha waited for him to return her gaze, but he could only look down, as if mournfully.

The Queen wiped a tear as she peeled her now useless gown all the way off. She took a deep breath.

She had no idea how she was going to explain her way out of this tomorrow, but she trusted Max to handle it. He said he would never let anything happen to her. She had no choice but to believe him.

* * *

Queen Asha rolled over in the bed of Max's man cave the next morning, sore and exhausted. She was regretting that second go-round after the swimming lesson now.

She groaned. "Think I could get away with faking a headache with the King tonight?"

She waited for a response. Until she realized she never before had to wait for a response from Mazigh.

When she turned to find that she was in bed alone, it worked better than a shot of espresso.

She sat up, looking around the cavernous space for signs of anything that could give her a sense of time. There were no clocks to speak of. Certainly no windows, so the sun could've been up already or not at all. She was supposed to be getting married tomorrow. Or... today?

"Max?" her voice echoed through the expanse. Perhaps he was upstairs.

"Emir??" she tried in a slightly less confident voice.

She cringed. The heady emotions of last night were waning and reality was setting in.

As much as she would love for the ringing bells of her intuition to have any bearing on what was about to happen today— which was marrying a man she didn't love— it was best for her to stay objective. She didn't even feel safe enough to process a single sexual thing that'd happened last night.

She took a deep breath, lay back down, and tried to inhale his lingering scent on the pillows, preparing for it to be her last chance.

"I love you," she whispered, willing herself off the bed and back into her dress from last night.

Suddenly she had a thought, so shocking in its horror that she stopped and stood up straight as though she'd heard a sound.

What if Max wasn't here because the King already found out? And administered justice?

What if she was next?

But then, she thought, surely the King would make an example of both of them. Either way, she thought it best to hightail it out of there as soon as she could.

"Max!" she cried one last time in the extravagant haven of the underground chateau. Her voice echoed off the walls until she was convinced she was all alone and started off for the mouth of the cave.

Once she made her way around the curve near the entrance, she could see that it was daylight. The sun wasn't high and unbearable so it must still be early, she deduced.

She started to feel guilty. Unless Max managed to send word somehow, her attendants were probably worried sick.

The boat. It was gone. So she couldn't leave if she wanted to.

Now she was really starting to freak out. Max knew that one night of learning the basics wasn't enough for her to make it across the water without a boat.

What if the King really was trying to punish her? Leave her here to starve? That would make an example of her.

But then she remembered that the King still needed her. If he cared about Ashwari at all, he would still at least need her to play the part of the Princess.

She could only hold on to the truth about his blind affection for her.

Suddenly she heard a rumbling in the distance, and not long after she heard it, she saw it. A boat.

Only this was one considerably bigger and with a motor. Not quite a yacht, but big enough to entertain in style. She shielded her eyes from the glare of the sun but she couldn't see who was driving it.

Her chief attendant Zara became visible the closer they got. The boat pulled right up to the dock and lowered a retractable metal ladder. Instantly, two other attendants appeared and made their way to her while Zara barked Arabic orders.

They knew where she was, but they'd asked no questions.

Max could've sent for them in secret. The way they shuffled

around her could be out of guilt rather than haste.

But the likelihood they would betray their King for a woman they barely knew... it was much more likely they bowed their heads and pretended not to know why she was alone on an island wearing the same dress from yesterday because they revered and respected their King, not her.

Her hope returned as the conclusion became obvious. Max really was the king.

They fast-walked her to the boat where she was whisked below deck to a luxurious room. A dress she presumed to be her wedding dress lay on the bed. She'd had no say in the dress, but luckily it was beyond anything she could've ever picked out for herself.

She was told gold was the traditional color of wedding gowns in this region, but the King must've put in a word with the dressmakers because the dress was a soft dim white. It was enmeshed in lace across the midriff, back, and sleeves. The luxurious embroidery and beadwork were so intricate they made it look simple. She couldn't believe what they were able to pull off in a matter of days. The royal dressmakers must've worked day and night.

She was shoved into a bathroom and stripped. The hot water was already running. Perhaps she really had been running late.

She realized she had no idea how this ceremony even operated. It's not as though she'd had a rehearsal.

"Does anyone know what time it is?" Asha ventured a question in English. She'd been attempting to learn Arabic and frowned that she hadn't thought to learn something as simple as "do you have the time."

One of her young helpers looked doe-eyed and rushed out, presumably to get Zara to answer her. It must've been pretty late because she was being scrubbed to death, hastily put in a robe, and primped like a pony for a show with a servant at the end of each limb.

Zara came rushing around the corner. Queen Asha kept her head still as she looked up.

"What time is it, Zara?"

"The Queen is due underneath the wedding canopy in one hour."

"One hour seems plenty of time to dress."

"Indeed, my Queen," Zara didn't argue.

"I should apologize for disappearing last night."

"You seemed distraught my Queen," Zara answered cryptically.

"I was. But I'm... better now."

Asha didn't know how to proceed. Zara's polite words weren't helping her piece together this puzzle.

"Did... Max tell you where I was this morning?"

Zara looked puzzled. "Max, your Majesty?"

"Mazigh."

"No, my queen. The King's Guard informed us of your whereabouts."

Queen Asha's heart sank. That was not the answer she wanted.

She could, of course, go "hey Zara, which one of these motherfuckers is which??" but she wasn't quite ready to make a fool of herself just yet.

Stupid fake kings and their advisors. Her heart rose and fell against her will again and again as she held still for hair and her makeup, which for some reason she wasn't permitted to see. She could hardly care about any of it.

She was warring between hope and bitter realism. The suspense alone might kill her dead. From what she understood there would be no aisle to walk down. The bride waited for the groom to appear in Manafi weddings.

"You should go to the bathroom now, my Queen," Zara urged.

"I already went."

"Go again."

She didn't even feel the boat come to a stop when they pulled up on the palace shore. Instead of docking in the same secluded spot the small dingy had been in, it stopped right in front of a beach that overlooked the palace courtyard, where the wedding canopy was already set up and guests were mingling and singing songs as they waited.

The guests were a breathtaking sea of colors, both in garments and skin tone. The women were covered in patterns and stripes, the men in neutral turbans and wraps. Colorful large umbrellas dotted the crowd and covered guests by the dozen. The pervasive presence of cell phones by nearly everyone cut through the traditional landscape like the surrealism of a movie set.

"It is time, my Queen," her attendant took her by the hand.

Asha emerged from below deck ten deep, her posse surrounding her on either side as they disembarked, one by one down the narrow staircase, Queen Asha in back.

When she got to the ladder at the front of the boat she could see there was a small white tent sitting on a pair of long sticks.

"What on Earth is that?"

"A palanquin, your Majesty."

"I'm supposed to get in that?"

"Yes, my Queen. A royal tradition. Have you ever been in one?"

"Of course not."

"It's pretty brilliant, your Majesty."

"You guys are really going to carry me?"

"The Royal Guard will escort you to the wedding tent, my Queen," Zara chuckled.

Her attendants walked beside the palanquin that carted her to the canopy made of white lace and adorned with soft pillows. It was royally enchanting AF but she could hardly luxuriate in it or even pay attention.

The guards lowered her to the ground in front of the ceremonial terrace that had also been hastily built. Zara extended a hand for her to take and guided her underneath the canopy where she sat on one of the elaborate pillows, her legs underneath her.

She sat and took a breath, waiting as the mingling continued. She recognized the King and Queen of Ghassan among the guests. Queen Kimberly raised a glass of empathetic knowing in her direction and she smiled, though the Queen likely couldn't have seen it under her imposing veil made of gold chainlink and beads. She added a timid wave just in case.

She longed for her family and tried not to get emotional thinking about them. Not that she would want them here for this particular soap opera.

Her legs began to tingle from lack of circulation but she didn't dare move. She grew hot under the veil, but the breeze underneath the canopy was pleasant and forgiving.

Finally, she saw the one she knew as the King out of the corner of her eye emerging from the palace. He was sharply dressed in a bright white tunic under a tailored black coat that looked more military than matrimonial. A black turban with a large jeweled pin and covered his hair. There was a large curved dagger in his belt.

He slowly came down the palace courtyard steps, also with a small entourage.

Her heart felt heavy as they approached. The King was front

and center as the others were in V formation behind him, their movements in sync. Each one of them looked dashing, especially the King leading the pack. He looked distinguished. Handsome. But he was not the one she wanted.

She instantly noticed that with every step that was taken, the guests paid them virtually no heed. Her whole body went cold and back to hot intermittently as the crew made their way down the aisle, and it made her stop breathing. Shivers attacked her, her chest heaved, only now for the opposite reason.

Her new theory had been right. He wasn't the King. No way was he the king. She found a piece of flesh at her ankle and pinched it relentlessly to make sure she was indeed awake.

She'd only been in Manaf three days, and that was enough. Even she garnered more attention when she got up to go to the bathroom.

No. He wasn't the king. Which, could most likely only mean one thing.

The disorientation of the moment blurred her vision. Her mind grasped for meaning, for direction. She searched her memory as the one she thought was the king all this time drew closer.

In the States, of course, they could've told her anything, couldn't they? But how could they have fooled her here? In Manaf?

It dawned on her that this must be the first time she could've ever observed the way others would treat this man who she thought was the King. Otherwise, she would've figured it out as fast as she had just done.

Today must be the first day that all three of them would be in the company of others. Except for the farewell dinner with her family, where no one could've been the wiser.

They kept the ruse going in Manaf by isolating her until this moment. The two men were only together with her behind closed doors. Max always dismissed their attendants before he visited. It wasn't just a matter of privacy, bordering on the inappropriate.

And the palace hadn't just allowed it because they had developed a rapport. Or because Max was so close to the King. They wouldn't. Only the King could get away with such behavior.

So if Max was really the King then... who was this guy coming to stand in front of her?

"Max?" she lowly uttered, looking up from her sitting position as he came to stand beside her on the King's side. He gave her a warm apologetic smile and his ebony eyes glittered.

"Mazigh, my Queen. No one has ever called me Max," he winked.

Don't call me that, Max would say. She'd wanted to use his whole name, as a sign of affection, but he'd sharply refused it.

Because Mazigh was his advisor's name.

Queen Asha gripped one of her many pillows, swaying, desperate to simply lay down in relief.

He wasn't just King of her heart. Max was Emir. Max was the King of Manaf.

Her memory went back to the day he showed up at her house. The two of them riding around Tampa, him showing up at the nursing home. Mrs. Nader.

All those times he appealed to her on behalf of the King, to see him beyond what she thought was his rejection... each time he'd been pleading on behalf of himself.

As predicted, Gabby dissolved into tears, a variety of emotions in them. That whole time, he was Him. And she was right.

She was right and she was gonna kill him.

"The King approaches!" a far-off voice shouted. Everyone was hushed as they craned their necks behind them.

Her sobbing echoed conspicuously in the quiet, at least in her own ears. She felt the energy of the crowd as she carried on, some of them touched with her emotional display, some of them troubled. Perhaps they perceived her tears as the anguish of a woman marrying a stranger. Before last night, they would've been.

Queen Asha saw the King coming, wearing a similar military-style tunic that was white, a long white turban on his head, the galloping of the white horse he was riding exploded in her ears.

She smiled between sobs underneath her veil. She kinda thought he looked ridiculous. They probably both looked ridiculous. If there were any doubt that they were the royals, the wardrobe took it all away.

He drew closer and dismounted his horse with a swing of his long leg and made his way down the aisle to where she lounged. She watched in disbelief as he drew closer and closer, until he was so close that his face was gone from view. The sandals on his dark feet were caked with white sand.

Suddenly he was sitting down beside her. He relinquished the turban once he got underneath the canopy. She couldn't believe the sight of him next to her, now and forever, his visage blurred from behind her linen veil and teary eyes.

"*My King and my husband*," she uttered the Manafi wedding ceremonial words in Farsi as practiced, not knowing what they meant. It was his turn to lift her veil and accept her.

The veil lifted up with a gesture of his arms, a stern look on his face. His eyes softened as he took in the sight of her and a pair of fresh tears fell. He smiled.

He placed a gentle hand under her eyes, wiping the water away before giving her a kiss on the cheek.

The wedding guests erupted in cheers and songs. The ceremony was officially complete.

15

Chapter 15

While the duo posed in picture after picture, the wedding guests were treated to a parade that ended at the palace banquet room and didn't conclude until the King and Queen were introduced and the reception began.

The celebration was raucous. The sunlight poured in from the high windows facing west, the sky looking artificially blue from the glass dome up above. Plates of food as numerous as the number of chairs to be filled lined every aisle of long tables that filled the banquet hall. The King and Queen sat next to each other at the front of the room, a bit removed from the revelry.

She was surprised to find a similar custom of meeting and greeting that they have in American weddings. The couple smiled, bowed, shook hands with whoever came up to greet them, depending on their rank.

Mazigh stood at the King's right, formerly presenting every person that approached. Not only did it look fancy, it probably had the added bonus of refreshing the King's memory, in case he'd forgotten who they were.

"The honorable Hakeem Abaj and his wife..."

Queen Asha looked on in quiet astonishment, watching people on the outside of their relationship give Max the respect and reverence reserved for King Khoury, before directing polite reverence toward her. How long before Max and Emir would merge in her mind?

Knowing that the years would melt this feeling away, she enjoyed the separation for the time being.

She, of course, always felt that he was deserving. But it turned out so did everyone else.

"Prime Minister Dicci," Mazigh droned. The King stood from his chair and bowed. He must be pretty important.

The King's attendants and advisors sat at his left, the Queen's on her right. Some of them had gotten up to join in the dancing and drinking that was going on. For a ceremony that seemed to be compulsively focused on their matrimony, virtually no one was paying attention now as the King sat leisurely in front of his meal.

The Queen looked poised where she sat. Demure at first glance, but at second or third, one might get the impression that she was distracted.

King Khoury gnawed on his bread as he sat back and looked at her intently. She looked completely different from the sexual being he'd unleashed last night. Certainly nothing like the girl Gabby that he'd met only ten days ago, wearing peasants' clothes and a proud demeanor.

She was dressed head to toe in linen white, dark makeup on her eyes and lips to dramatize her deep cocoa color. He felt the envy of other men clouding the room. She looked like a Queen. One that was marrying a stranger.

She didn't seem pleased to be married to him and he was

giddy inside to know that this would've been her inevitable appearance, no matter who her husband was.

Though, right now she could be forgiven for being standoffish towards him. Even though he'd confessed his love to her last night, he'd yet to give her a reason to trust him.

He imagined the more that she grew to trust him, the more the wall would come down. This too made him giddy to think about.

"You look disturbed, my Queen," he quietly nudged her.

She kept her face neutral, beautiful. "I am disturbed."

He smirked. "May I ask why?"

"You made a mockery of me."

His smirk waned. "I did no such thing."

"I've been trying to forget the last 12 hours. Trying to forget last night ever happened. So that I could do this job."

The smirk returned, blooming to a smile. "And what job is that?"

"Being a Queen."

"Being Mazigh's Queen," he corrected.

"And him," Queen Asha stirred her anger, nodding in Mazigh's direction. "How could he have gone along with this charade?"

"It was his idea," the King divulged. "However, he played the role much longer than he wanted, I'll admit."

"'Longer than he wanted,'" the Queen quoted. "So there was a structure to this plan?"

"...A loose one." The King's eyes crinkled, a way of smiling she'd only seen from him a few times.

"We have a few more, your Majesty," Mazigh broke in.

"Of course," the King replied, seeing a familiar face. His expression brightened.

"The King and Queen of Ghassan," Mazigh arbitrarily announced.

King Khoury smiled, greeting him with a distinguished bow. "You came."

"I told you we would. The Queen wouldn't let me forget," King Hafiz mused.

"I couldn't miss the big reveal," Queen Kim widened her eyes. Queen Asha stiffened.

Did she mean... Max's true identity?

Shit. Gabby forgot about her hysterical confessions the night that she stayed with them, after the man she thought was the King admitted to faking documents in order to kidnap her.

He must've told them to keep his little charade going. Gabby turned to her husband accusingly. He scrunched his face a bit in guilt. Bel laughed.

"You had them in on it too??" Asha accused.

"It was the King's idea," Kim blurted, elbowing her husband.

King Hafiz was flabbergasted. "I simply told him to find some excuse to be in the States, not channel Eddie Murphy," Bel said.

Queen Kimberly cackled cartoonishly, inadvertently thawing Queen Asha's fury. She could only look at Kim and shake her head in shared helplessness over their silly husbands.

"I thought it was a little weird that you were spending sooo much time with Mazigh," Kim recalled. Asha lowered her head, her hands to her temples in embarrassment. The two Kings chuckled uncontrollably.

They seemed to make a good unit, Emir thought. He looked forward to being able to go on couple's outings with his friend.

"How long can you stay?" Khoury asked.

"As long as we're welcome."

"Then be our honored guests tonight. Did you bring your

sons?"

"We did."

"Very well. The car we borrowed last week will be ready for you tomorrow."

Bel grabbed his hand in a firm shake, a sincere look of happiness in his eye. "Congratulations, my friend."

"Thank you," Emir nodded stoically.

The couples exchanged kisses with the bride as another wave of foot traffic waited patiently behind to greet them.

The Queen returned her eyes lazily to the reception during the lull. "Just when exactly did you plan on telling me the truth?"

"I wrote you a letter. You were supposed to get it during the binding ceremony."

"Why didn't I?"

"Because no one could find you," he said. The Queen sighed sheepishly, having no rebuttal.

"I wanted to suss you out," the King explained. "While also getting you back to Manaf safely. Obviously, the truth could not remain hidden forever."

"Nonsense. You liked making a fool of me. Otherwise, you would've come clean last night."

"I wanted your passion," he openly confessed. The party was just loud enough that no one could hear their bickering.

"Even if it meant being someone you weren't? Even if I was terrified? That being with you would get me killed?"

Suddenly the King's hand was sliding underneath her skirts in a flash, under the table, beyond the gaze of the wedding guests as he turned his body towards her.

Queen Asha could do nothing but stare back at him and try to keep her revving heart from leaving her breathless.

She could barely believe what was happening. This side of

Max... the King... she'd only known for nearly a day. And nothing to this extent. His eyes were so stern it intimidated her.

But then the King's hand drifted up and up and she didn't know how to feel. His touch became feather-soft on her flesh. Her face softened. This side of *herself* was equally just as foreign.

"Hearing you describe your inner-struggling gives me anguish. And I am sorry. But I regret nothing. Feeling you give way underneath me was a thrill no one has ever been able to give me," he lowly confessed. "Your King is forever indebted to the Queen for it."

She swallowed, her head swimming, but she found her words. "I've been trying to forgive the King since we landed here. But it's you I should be forgiving."

"*I* am the King."

"So you admit you lied. About the passport. The visa."

The King sighed through his nostrils, as though losing patience. "Enough, my Queen. It is done."

"But I am not. Your Majesty," Queen Asha insisted respectfully, though she didn't flinch from his black gaze.

The King's lips went to her ear, leaning over to her. His long fingers inched up until they were wedged between her legs underneath the table. Her legs gave slightly, to further accommodate him.

Her cheeks were on fire as her fingers gripped the table, trying to contain her energy. Their attendants were starting to pretend not to look at them.

"I want you to tell me all about your grievances when we leave here," the King said.

"You don't mean that," she breathed.

"I do," his voice oozed, "I've thought of nothing else but this moment since we met."

"To say you ruined 'this moment' last night is an under-statement," she said, speaking of her thoroughly demolished virginity.

The King chuckled devilishly. "Is that what this is about? Had you imagined your wedding night since you were a girl?"

"Can you even go a single day without humiliating me?"

He straightened up to look at her again. She was genuinely angry with him, genuinely hurt by him.

The hand below the table relented and smoothed out her skirts. The hand that was above the table grabbed her by the chin and gave her a chaste kiss on her lips. The banquet hall was instantly uproarious with clinking glass and chauvinist men banging their tables. King Khoury's lip curled into a smirk.

"You are foolish to think I have ever had the upper hand over you, my Queen. My behavior even now only proves this. Ask Mazigh yourself, if I've ever done something so ridiculous."

"How long do we have to be here?" Asha lowly asked.

The King's gaze bored through her. He saw the lust dulling her eyes and realized he was indeed an asshole for bringing her body to life the night before her wedding.

He'd hoped to enjoy Gabby's smiles today if all went well. But the admittedly impressive ceremony was hard to enjoy with the mounting new addiction infecting her blood.

He felt a pang of guilt, but only a little one. With considerably more experience than her, he knew their simmering attraction was unusual.

He held her delicately by the hand. He kissed it.

"We have a few more guests to greet," the King said, looking up from his high-backed chair.

"General Togbe Olayinka, supreme leader of Ashwari," said Mazigh.

Gabby's body locked in terror at the announced name. She didn't dare look at the face. Not yet.

"General..." She heard her husband's voice above her somewhere like a cloud, felt him leaning over to give the General's hand a shake, the one that had just been under her skirts.

"Emir," came the General's gravelly tenor, the first time she'd ever heard someone other than her use his first name. And it wasn't out of affection.

"Thank you for accepting my invitation on such short notice. I know your religious advisors frown upon participating in such extravagant affairs such as this," the King continued cordially. Calm.

His calmness caused Asha's shoulders to slowly inch back down. She stealthily slinked her hand into his as the two spoke.

"Nonsense. My mother would shame me if I didn't attend the wedding of Awate's son."

"And how is your mother?" Emir sternly asked.

"She's passed. Not long after your mother, may she rest," the General nodded.

"May she rest."

The General turned his attention toward Asha and her blood chilled as he stopped staring and smiled. He was a heavyset man, but tall. With one gray eye and one brown one. As dark-skinned as the King and showing few signs of his age.

"I'm eager to meet your lovely bride."

"General Olayinka, meet Queen Asha Gabrielle Otieno Khoury, daughter of Oba Otieno."

There was a beat of tense silence between the two men, so tense that Gabby wanted simply to hide under the table.

She got the feeling that this was the first official reveal of her name. Clearly, it rang some bells for the man.

She didn't even look over at her husband's face, though she could only guess that his stern, majestic look was beating out Olayinka's plastered smile. The Queen remained poker-faced, legs crossed in her high back chair, trying to breathe slow.

"You bear an astonishing resemblance to someone I used to know," General Olayinka said, holding out his hand as if to offer a kiss to hers.

Asha tightly gripped the arms of her chair, eyeing his hand as though it were a cobra. She heard his laughter.

"My, my. She's magnificent, your Majesty. It seems my asset in the States has taught her well."

King Khoury's air was towering, and not just because of the high platform that sat on. "I invited you here as a courtesy, General. Don't make me regret that."

"The courtesy of a pretender? Who tries to usurp my country with an imposter?"

"So you understand what's happened here today," the King bellowed without malice.

"I understand that you want to declare war. If you wanted my modest little sliver of Africa there are less treacherous ways to go about it."

King Khoury didn't argue semantics. "This seemed more efficient."

Another staredown passed before Olayinka continued. "I hope you have not paid your source for this so-called 'intelligence' you have received. She and my asset have deceived you in the most insidious way. Invoking the name of his daughter? *Qutmabreshe!* You would pour disgrace on the tragedy of the family of my Lord? Who was my mentor?"

"As if you had no hand in it. How dare you," Queen Asha responded curtly with a scowl.

General Olayinka did not take his eyes off the King to address Gabby, but she looked squarely at him.

"Ask your *mentor's* trusted commander beside you if the baby Asha could be found in the palace when he was given his orders," King Khoury said in a low tone. "Ask him if a girl of similar age belonging to one of the maidservants was put in her place."

A look of recollection mixed with horror flashed faintly over Olayinka's face.

He looked over at the Queen again, truly looking at her. And now he was starting to pale as if he'd seen a ghost.

His mind was stuck in that fateful day, rage and adrenaline coursing through him over every little deviation of the plan. The people would never forgive the beheadings he thought, remembering how he reamed his Commander. The Queen hadn't been back a day and now they weren't fit for proper burial. Now he would have to lean into his ruthlessness, convince the people it was necessary.

The thought had stubbornly kept him awake for years. Why would he behead them? Burn the bodies? It had been his restless intuition, he now knew.

"If you wanted to betray my family right, you should have done it yourself," Queen Asha broke through his thoughts, an eyebrow slowly raising and lowering as though she read his mind.

Gabby didn't know this man from Adam, but somehow she was certain that if he was in private, Olayinka would be lining up his men right now and shooting them until he calmed down long enough to come up with a plan. Knew it like she knew her own body.

But here, he was no threat and he knew it.

"They warned me about you, *Malik Shab*. That the cub of a

215

wolf is still a wolf. I invited you into my home."

"You mean *my* home, General," the Queen interjected.

"Ashwari will never accept you," he replied to King Khoury, indignant. "Ashwari is no longer under monarchy rule and will not return to it. We will fight. Fight and win. As we have done once before."

"Ashwari will be a democracy," Gabby flatly countered his deluded tirade. That got his attention.

King Khoury stiffened. He wasn't supposed to know that yet.

Olayinka gave her a sickening look at her outburst. He clearly had a distaste for Queens inserting themselves in matters of Kings.

"Says *you*, imposter?" the General spat.

"Says the Queen of Ashwari, surviving daughter of the rightful ruler of Ashwari, King Oba Otieno. Once the King of Manaf has helped me remove the usurper," Queen Asha shot back without moving a muscle.

King Khoury was going to eat her for dessert. The Cave was definitely happening again tonight.

He squeezed her hand, noticing they were beginning to draw attention. "The guests, my love."

Olayinka kept his gaze on Gabby. "You should watch out, Khoury. It hasn't been a week of playing dress-up and already the American has let her title go to her head."

Emir cracked a smile, for the sake of the reception, but also because he was genuinely amused.

"She was like this when I met her, General," he replied. The General kept a disrespectful eye on his bride, but King Khoury didn't correct him. She was poised, pissed, and winning the staredown.

If he had any doubts before now, they were all gone. She was the Princess.

"Your father was no more a rightful King than I am, young one," the General finally said, conceding to the reality that he was seeing before him. Otieno's daughter had indeed survived. He leaned in as if confiding a great secret.

"Ashwari is bathed in blood," he said.

He cut his eyes back to the King. A sickly smile came across his lips.

"Congratulations again, your Majesty. And good luck."

The King and Queen watched as he slowly sauntered out of the banquet hall with a small detail in military uniform that had gathered by the door.

The guests tried not to conspicuously watch their exit. All except Bel, who had kept his eyes on Emir from the banquet hall tables.

Emir had his eyes on Gabby, who merely looked down at her dinner plate still full of food that was currently being pushed around by the fork in her hand. She was still getting used to it. Her head maidservant had apparently told the kitchen that she liked the fried bread.

He was going to strip her naked, wrap his arms around her and bury himself inside her until his mind was irretrievable.

King Khoury caught the eye of Mazigh. He nodded to one of his men who sent another over. The man stood behind the King and stooped in front of his ear.

He whispered something briefly and the man advanced directly into the center of the reception and clapped his hands twice.

"The King and Queen will now retire to the wedding chamber!" he announced. The banquet hall instantly cheered.

The King regally stood and extended his hand to Queen Asha,

who accepted it politely and took hold of her train with the other hand. Asha followed his lead up the stairs behind them, up a grand staircase where ululating and uproar could still be heard well after they had disappeared from view.

16

Chapter 16

The King's chambers were twice as large as her own. As she made her way across the expansive room she was surprised to see the view from his balcony included her own balcony. Though she shouldn't have been.

"Seems a little weird to be having our honeymoon directly above the wedding reception," she said, looking across the room at his massive terrace.

"Be grateful that I am not the King of Ghassan," he replied. The King watched her in her queenly garb, hardly able to believe what he was seeing. It seemed like a million years had passed since he first laid eyes on her. Her long hair hung in a cascade below her shoulders. The bangles on her legs and wrists jangled and the heavy fabric of her train ruched with her every step.

"Was the ceremony not to your satisfaction?" he prodded her.

"Everything was wonderful," the Queen curtly admitted.

He slowly advanced toward her. "You have my permission to speak freely."

"Thank goodness for that," she sarcastically replied.

"Princess—"

"Why would you invite him?"

"So he could be here and not there." He replied. Asha kicked off her soft shoes in an unamused scoff. "I wanted him to hear the news directly from us both. Catch him off guard and assess his reaction."

"What asset was he going on about?"

"I believe he is trying to suggest that you were planned as a plant for me."

"Well that's a 25 year long game for that ass," Gabby widened her eyes sarcastically. "My wedding day has been fraught with ambush."

"Don't be angry with me, my Queen," he sighed, hoping to butter her up. "The more our relationship... progressed, the harder it was to come clean."

"So you figured you might as well wait until the inevitable?"

He slowly closed the distance between them. "I was convinced that you already knew."

"No, I didn't. I didn't even suspect it until last night. And the hope was... unbearable."

He slinked his arm around her and enveloped her. Her hands were on his chest.

"I was going to tell you once we left for Manaf. When you found out about the fake passport, I didn't anticipate how you would react. You already felt betrayed, I couldn't add to it," he said, feeling along her bodice for a zipper as he kissed her neck. Instead, he found about a million buttons. "I didn't anticipate how much I would grow to care for you. Or that you would care for me. Or that it would positively melt my heart."

"Did you mean what you said last night?" Queen Asha asked, his shoulders at her eye-level.

"I said many things last night," the King said with naked eyes.

"Refresh my memory."

"Does the King... do you... is the King truly blind with affection for me?" she glanced upward.

He saw a glimpse of the girl Gabby peaking through all the Queen's many adornments. His emotions nearly overcame him.

"All the King sees is you. Whether his eyes are open or closed. When he wakes up, when he sleeps."

"Why?" she asked in a confounded whisper.

Emir could no longer hold back. He kissed his wife's lips, again and again, rhythmic and deep. He reached for the single clasp and her sash loosened. It fell to the floor in one piece.

"You left me this morning," she said when they finally broke apart.

"I know. I am sorry," he cooed. He found her ear and whispered, "I have many more things to teach you tonight, my Queen."

"About that, your Majesty," she breathed.

He smiled. "Yes?"

"I was planning to beg the King's forgiveness this evening."

"For?" he asked, starting on the buttons on her lower back.

"Well, you see, I had a bit of a late night last night."

"Is that so?" he replied, intrigued, making quick headway, her dress giving way. "Was this... after you had my entire palace grounds looking for you?"

"Yes... what happened with that, by the way?" Gabby wondered.

"My most trusted advisor handled it."

"Seriously?"

"Indeed," said the King, peeling her sleeves down. She wore a strapless brassiere. "He heard us arguing on the terrace, but once he entered the room we were gone. We were the only two missing. Along with my boat. He knows what that means."

"Wow," the Queen muttered. "He's a beast."

"Doing what?"

"Pardon?"

"You said you were up late last night. What were you doing?" he asked as her skirt came down. Her underwear was skimpy lace.

"...Anticipating this moment, my King," Gabby replied diplomatically.

"Ah. Nerves?" he played along. He abruptly scooped her up in his big arms as though she were a feather. She let out an unexpected squeal.

"...Something like that," she giggled.

"The Queen must be exhausted," he said, half on autopilot as he carried her the short distance to his impossibly large bed covered in dark crimson with gold damask.

"I am," she sighed. "And also sore. From... anticipating." He kissed her hand in sympathy.

"Well," he said looming over her, "it's natural for the Queen to be nervous on her wedding night, of course."

"Yes, I am very nervous. I have never done any of this," she playfully lied.

"Very well. The King will abstain from consummation tonight," he said, removing his heavy white coat. She watched him undressing from the bed, already down to her underwear. She nervously smiled. A hand was behind her head and one leg bent as he eyed her.

"You're too magnanimous, my King," she cooed.

"You will pleasure your King in other ways."

A smile curled up her lip. "Your Majesty—"

"And you will do me the honor of letting me pleasure you until

I've had my fill."

Asha gnawed her lip nervously. He let his trousers down and she was once again confronted with the King's anaconda. She imagined that it would take her years to adjust to the sight. She licked her lips, but she could no longer feel them.

"Husband—"

"I like hearing you call me that," he said, having climbed onto the bed and over her body. He feasted his eyes on her until it made her heart flutter. He kissed her pouty lips, her chin, down her neck.

"May I call you by your given name, my King?" she moaned.

His lips found her ear. "You may only call me Emir while my cock is deep inside you," he lowly ordered.

Her eyes popped open and followed his as he again kissed her lips. "Of course, your Majesty."

"But there's no need to worry about that tonight."

"Thank you, husband," she replied between kisses, regretting her request a bit now.

"Have you ever seen a cock, my Queen?" he inquired.

"No, your Majesty."

"Are you lying?"

"I would never, your Majesty," she insisted without a flinch.

"You're being a little too convincing now, young Asha."

"You love it."

"I do," he nodded as he chuckled. He slinked down her frame until he'd made it to her stomach, where he couldn't help skimming with his lips. She squirmed under him as he got to her navel, and finally to her lacy underwear. He hiked up one leg and slowly lapped at the stiff fabric covering her sex.

Gabby didn't know whether to sit up and watch, or grab his head like a glorious joystick and enjoy the view from the King's balcony doors.

She felt his finger parting the fabric, up and down like chains on a zipper. She felt one kiss, another, then his mouth engulfed her clit. She let out a moan and looked down.

"My vizier seemed to disappear not long after you did last night, Queen Asha. Care to confess anything?"

"No, my King," she sighed. The sight, sound, and sensation of his tongue on her sex filled her senses.

"But you were with him," he bellowed.

"Of course."

"You don't deny it?" he asked, looking up from his task.

"He's devoted to you, my King. Not to me," she insisted.

"You want him," he accused. Then his pink tongue found her clit and she realized she was dealing with a sex god. Instantly her arousal began turning colors and she couldn't hold her head up anymore.

"No," she denied groggily.

"You let him make love to you," he accused.

"No," she whimpered. Tortuously his pace languished. His hands roamed her thighs.

"Oh God, don't stop..." she begged.

"You want to come?"

"Yes."

"Say it like I taught you."

"It's yours not his..." she moaned again and again, until orgasm was spasming her muscles and she folded inward, her strapless brassiere still in place as she flopped all over the King's velvety sheets.

He'd forgotten his concession midway through Queen Asha's orgasm. He couldn't wait to grab her boneless body by the middle and flip her face down ass up. He shivered thinking about the way her body had taken him eagerly for the first time in this position only last night.

Gabby let the King position her like a puppet, euphoric and more than happy to let him break his promise of going easy on her tonight. She loved that she could make him turn sloppy and she craved the feeling like a drug.

The cool air on her naked body felt as thick as a blanket. She moaned in her post-orgasmic bliss, feeling the pressure of him at her slick entrance. She had the same feeling of being stretched to capacity, her insides seemed to shift upward around him in response.

Smoothly he went in and in. Her waist disappeared between his big hands and their bodies locked. Gorgeous velvety bliss shimmered across her as his hips began to move. She felt good enough to pass out.

"Emir..." she moaned, almost like a curse or a warning, and it confirmed what he already knew. He was deep inside her. He curled his fingers around her middle.

"Say it again, my Queen..."

"Emir..."

"No, the other thing," he panted.

"It's yours, not his..."

The honeymoon lovemaking gave him a different kind of high. If last night was about two lovers, hungry and forbidden, tonight was about two countries, legitimate and sacred. Political.

"I think I'm gonna come..." she breathed.

"You're so beautiful, my love..."

Asha was finally his, which meant Ashwari was his. He thought about it as he rubbed her round backside, receiving him over and over. Her face contorted as he pounded, her moans of pleasure frantic, even as she was still inching away, hesitant to receive all of him. He was penetrating Ashwari, filling up and impregnating Ashwari.

The Queen gripped the sheets as she focused. "My King... I'm coming... I'm coming..."

"Asha!" he groaned.

He was already contemplating round two as he climaxed in record time, slowly jetting into her while looking down at her lithe, diminutive form.

* * *

"Did you ever meet my parents?" Queen Asha asked amid the quiet, the King and Queen having spent the whole night intertwined. The Queen lay on his chest enjoying the cool desert air from the terrace.

"Once," he revealed, perusing his memory, eyes closed. "Before I was king."

"So you must've been very young," she marveled.

"I was. I met you as well."

"You didn't," she scoffed in disbelief.

"I did. I held you."

"You didn't!" she raised her head, eyes wide.

King Khoury laughed.

"It's true."

Gabby refused to believe that they'd ever met before now. "Swear on your entire kingdom."

"I can show you the room where the nurse kept you. You were very well behaved."

She sounded emotional, touched as she cooed "Emir..."

She wasn't supposed to call him that if they weren't having sex. But he couldn't care less about it now. He never knew he missed having a name until she called it.

"How else were we betrothed? Informally, anyway."

"Why am I just now hearing about this?"

"Because you just now asked."

"What else can I ask?"

"What else would you like to know?"

"How many others have there been?"

Emir chuckled, instantly knowing what she was after. "Ask me a different one."

"I have a right to know," she insisted.

"That's debatable, Princess."

"Queen, you mean?"

"But I like calling you Princess."

"Very well," she conceded. She had her head resting on her hand, which was on his chest, eyeing him. "Any of my attendants?"

"I would never disrespect you by putting one of these women near the palace."

"So what, you had them all killed?" she scoffed.

"How could you be worried about such things at a time like this?"

"I don't know," Gabby fiddled with the twisted-up hairs in the middle of his mostly smooth chest. "The matriarchs said that you and Mazigh had... a reputation."

Emir sighed. "The King went through a phase," he said, referring to himself again in the third person. "I was tired, lonely, resentful. I had no safe ways of rebelling. I was heavily secluded and disciplined when it came to matters of Manaf. But once I came of age, it seemed as though everyone saw fit to expose me to debauchery. I eventually realized that they were afraid that perhaps I had no attraction to women."

Gabby shrunk down even more thinking of their confrontation last night when she ran away.

"It seemed every man allowed himself this indulgence if it was available. And they all paid a heavy price. Except for Mazigh. There was simply nothing Mazigh could do to lose his place in the world. And he knew it. Mazigh has been a slut for as long as I have known him."

The Queen laughed. "So you decided to become a student of his?"

"I tried. I tried to self-destruct. No one knows that to this day, not even Mazigh. They didn't know my mind. On the outside, I simply looked like a young man taking advantage of his great power. They approved of it."

"I think they were relieved."

"I was supposed to get it all out of my system and then settle down. My father married my mother at 21. But he wasn't faithful to her."

"How did your mother feel about your 'phase'?"

"She approved of it."

"Really?"

"The Queen Mother meant well. She thought she knew enough of men to raise me to be one. But her actions only proved how little she truly understood."

Gabby felt dwarfed by how little she knew of this man and his emotions as he spoke. "I snapped out of my rebellion and took my rightful place. My heart ached to finally become King so that she could be protected again. I was devoted to finding someone suitable, but it seemed she didn't exist."

"And then you found me."

"And then I found you."

"Do you miss her?" Gabby asked.

A violent warmth overcame him, so much that he nearly couldn't answer. A mix of joy and grief. He tamped it down within himself, as though it had come dislodged from wherever he contained it.

"Yes."

"Tell me something else."

"Like what?"

"Anything."

The King laughed. "Sex has piqued your curiosity?"

"I'm always curious about you, my love," she said in a velvety tone that he'd never heard. His heart felt like it was in a vacuum. He swallowed.

He had to be careful. She could put a bullet right between his eyes and he'd never see it coming, he suddenly realized.

But then he relaxed. If he couldn't trust Queen Asha then he wouldn't want to survive anyway.

"That's true, I suppose."

"Everyone kept saying that there's plenty of time to get to know you once we're married. And now we're married, so. Get to talking."

"Very well. You want to know something else about me?"

"Yes."

"...I need your help."

"With what?"

"With Ashwari," he admitted.

The Queen sat up on her elbow, realizing her transition to power. She'd been the Queen of Ashwari most of her life, though she'd only just found out. Now she was also Queen of Manaf.

And the King needed her, just as he'd explained when he was just Max to her.

"What can I do?"

King Khour smoothed the hair from her face with his fingers. "Defeating the General will not be difficult. In fact, the operation is underway as we speak."

At hearing that, Gabby's heart doubled. Obviously, he hadn't just been canoodling with her for the last 24 hours, but it was still strange to think of all the different facets of her husband, the King.

She felt both paranoid and ill-equipped as she heard him talk. This was her country they were discussing, after all. Could he have asked her permission to invade it?

"What will be difficult is maintaining Ashwari, once he is removed," he continued. "He is likely calling on his Muslim allies that surround the nation on every side."

"They're hardly a threat," she asserted confidently with only three days of foreign affairs under her belt. "They've made a spectacle out of vowing peace, so they can't lose the people. And only Zaire is larger than Manaf."

"And that is enough. They are twice the size collectively."

"Doesn't Manaf have allies? Saudi Arabia?"

"Allies that will back their Muslim enemies over their Christian friends. Especially if the Queen wants Ashwari to remain independent."

The Queen furrowed her brow in concern. What was he telling her?

"So then that's it? We're fucked? I left my country for nothing?" the Queen asked.

"Not necessarily," he persuaded. Emir sat up against the headboard. "There may be a way to protect Ashwari without angering Manaf's existing allies."

Gabby pondered. "The U.N.?"

"Better."

She raised an eyebrow. "The U.S.?"

The King nodded. "We are already in talks with the U.S. for an embassy. But obviously, I could tell them nothing about you while I was there. I'll need you to come with me to negotiations. So you can appeal to their... emotions."

"You need me to talk about being an illegal alien and cry on camera."

"...Something like that."

Gabby tossed her head in thought. "Won't this anger Manaf's allies?"

"A little," the King wrinkled his handsome face. "But things can stay amiable if we can convince them that Ashwari's independence was your idea."

"It was my idea."

"See? This will be easy," Khoury charmed her. She had a feeling he'd been preparing this little proposal for some time.

"You know, you didn't have to loosen me up with sex before you asked me to do this for you."

"Of course, my Queen," he said with a kiss.

"What did Mrs. Nader say to you?"

The King smiled. "She said 'I prayed for you every day and now you are here.'"

Queen Asha beamed. "And what did you say?"

"I thanked her and told her that she was blessed because the Queen of Ashwari was also in her midst."

"And then she prayed for you again."

He nodded. "She did."

17

Epilogue

The King and Queen of Manaf traditionally occupied separate parts of the palace. Gabby thought initially that she would positively hate such an arrangement, but so far, it didn't seem as restrictive as it sounded.

In the mornings the King was usually already gone. For such a tall, imposing King she could never catch his measured, deliberate movements up and out of the bed next to her. No matter how early the Queen attempted to wake she could never catch him. He would always send her attendants in after him, who woke the Queen in the mornings if she hadn't already awakened herself.

Most of his days were longer than hers, of course. He would either request her presence wherever he was, or visit her in the Queen's chambers if that's where she was.

It seemed a bit pompous and needy to make others track down her whereabouts and make the trek to find her and request her presence. There was such a thing as cell phones, after all. She was often in the middle of something and there was no indication that she couldn't answer back, "tell him to give me an hour."

But she got the sense this was frowned upon. And anyway, so far she'd been happy to comply with his request. In fact, she lived for it.

"The King requests the Queen's presence in the King's parlor, my Queen," said Zara.

"I heard," Queen Asha replied. She was starting to pick up some Arabic through the rote address of the servants. Though she still wasn't comfortable speaking it.

She was dragging her feet on this day, however, because she'd received word from her doctors that she was not yet pregnant.

She hadn't been feeling well a few nights ago, and naturally, Emir had assumed the inevitable. She hadn't spoken to him since she found out. And she assumed that if she'd been told the news, then she was probably the last to know.

But there were no signs of anything. And she was starting to entertain the dark irony that perhaps she was defective. What if Mazigh had been right about her being too old?

But when she got to the King's parlor there was nothing in his eyes beyond the usual loving affection as she sat down next to him, the scent of strong coffee already staining the air.

He usually continued sitting in silence once she arrived, pursuing the paper. He would summon her to cozy up next to him or grab her hand. Occasionally asking about her day or mood.

To say it was old-fashioned was an understatement. She herself usually had little to say. Otherwise, he entertained her thoughts quietly, not unlike their time spent as Max and Gabby.

"How has your family settled in?" he suddenly asked.

"Nicely."

After her diplomatic missions to Ashwari her family came back with her to visit and, of course, never left just as she predicted.

Her surrogate family enjoyed elevated standing in Ashwari as the Queen's royal kin and the previous Queen's allies. Her sister Mackenzie attended school in Manaf, while her brother Faraj had found a job with the new Ashwari government and had recently begun dating a girl there. One or all of them were routinely entertained at the palace, sometimes without the Queen ever knowing they were there until after the fact.

"Are you alright?"

Queen Asha took a deep breath and gave him a toothless smile cozying up next to him on the parlor's tufted leather Chesterfield. After a moment he was still waiting for her to come clean.

"I assume the doctor told you the news," she said.

"He did."

"Are you disappointed?"

"Of course I am. But it changes nothing."

"It's been a year. I'm afraid something's wrong with me."

"Well... the problem is not with you. That much I can tell you."

"What do you mean 'that much'?"

"I mean, that the doctor and I have spoken extensively today. And he suspects that the problem may lie with me."

Queen Asha sat up suddenly. Before she could go on he continued.

"He doesn't think it's likely to be serious. One sample will confirm his suspicions."

"And if it isn't? Serious?"

"Then it is a matter of a simple procedure."

"And what if it is more than that?"

The King gave her a loving gesture with his head. "One thing at a time, Princess."

234

* * *

Queen Asha instantly become the jewel of the Manaf culture once she set foot in the country as hardly more than a rumor, a mysterious American who'd won their beloved king's heart in record time. But once King Khoury had revealed her identity, it was as though all hell had broken loose.

News traveled slower in Ashwari. Yet they were the first to see Manafi troops traversing their country roads and conversing with locals as early as the day of the royal couple's wedding. They were told that King Otieno's daughter was alive and marrying the King of Manaf in a private ceremony. They were told to spread the news, as well as to stay away from the city. The firefight on the ground in Ashwari could be heard from the Queen's balcony.

"Would you like to know how your parents died, Princess Asha?"

General Olayinka spoke to the Queen while they stood in the midst of his luxurious palace, formerly her family's palace. And now the General's prison cell.

When King Khoury informed her of Olayinka's inevitable surrender and capture, she'd insisted on coming against his own wishes. But he knew from the determined look in her eye that he could not deny her the closure.

They showed up together to look upon the sight of the disgraced General, surrounded by Manafi guards. Not a single soldier or member of his cabinet lifted a finger to help him fight.

"It's *Queen* Asha, General. And I know how they died," she replied, proud-faced, holding tightly onto her husband's arm.

"You know of their inevitable demise, but not how they died," the General wheezed, looking otherwise defeated as he gleefully dangled the story over the Princess like bait, the last little joy he would probably ever know.

"Your father, he did not fight. When the civil unrest broke out, I had them sequestered to the palace on my orders. The King complied without hesitation. My Commander tells me it took several hours for him to realize what was happening."

Gabby fought back a peculiar onset of emotion for a man that she didn't know. One who was supposedly ruthless but that gave birth to her nonetheless.

"You sent others to betray his trust?"

"A fatal mistake, I realize now. Had I been there, I would have known immediately that whatever girl they found and put in your place wasn't you. I would not have left any loose ends."

The Queen smoothed out her yellow saree. The matching yellow headdress she wore betrayed her significant rank, the beehive shape of its ceremonial folds extending behind her head like a hieroglyph.

"I will let you choose your fate, General. Would you rather stand trial for your crimes? Or would you like to fight your way out of your own house, you and all who live here? As my family did?"

Olayinka's yellow eyes slowly rolled to face hers. "You have your father's ruthlessness."

"If justice can be called ruthlessness, then yes I do."

"Perhaps you should consult your husband first, Princess."

"Queen," she corrected him again. "*Your* Queen, General."

"Whatever you do to me will cause an international incident," he confidently threatened.

"Is that so? Well. Perhaps we will let the people of Ashwari decide then," Queen Asha replied. King Khoury relinquished an approving grin.

Three months later Gabby was back in the states, now a Queen.

She arrived in the exact opposite manner that she had left. Surrounded by guards, attendants, flashing camera bulbs, and requests to look this way and that.

Having spent time in her home country alongside her husband, helping to form a skeletal new government, drafting treaties, and selecting Manafi advisors to help the Ashwari people implement elections, she was looking every inch the leader of a nation that she actually was.

Her family hardly recognized her when she returned to the former home that seemed to her now as tiny as a shoebox. The family had prepared a meal of Gabby's favorite foods, anticipating her brief stop there on her way to the White House.

"Queen Gabby," her sister tearfully grinned as they hugged. Her mother simply held her cheeks with both hands as she sobbed. Her father gave King Khoury a firm handshake.

"Allow me the courtesy of apologizing to your family in person. For my earlier deception. Discretion was necessary."

By the time Gabby got around to remembering that her family could use the update, the story had just started to reach the American radar. She got on video chat with her sister once her identity was revealed.

"Gabby... what?!?" Mackenzie had begun, bewildered.

"What what?"

"Did you fucking *marry* the right-hand man?!"

Queen Asha laughed. She'd nearly forgotten about that exchange with her sister that night in her bedroom.

"We understand, your Majesty," Gabby's surrogate father beamed. "Forgive earlier our rudeness and our ignorance and we will be even."

"*I* knew," Gabby's mother beamed as she greeting the King in the same manner, with her hands on his cheeks as well. The

King smiled and everyone laughed.

"You did not, *Ema*," Mackinzie insisted.

"I knew that he was in love with her," her mother insisted.

"How?" Queen Asha grinned as she looked at her mother, curious. King Khoury's pulse quickened a bit in embarrassment.

"The day he came to take you to the one we thought was king. He looked at you the way he looks at you now," she revealed.

The Queen looked back at her husband with a loving look that made him melt. If he could turn red he would have.

Queen Asha's surrogate mother returned her hands to his cheeks. She added the sloppy kiss of a mother-in-law as the family laughed.

After freeing the Ashwari people, Gabby met with U.S. officials to personally request that they join Manaf in becoming an Ashwari ally. And with the public's eyes directly on the issue, the American government was under immense pressure to take the hidden princess seriously.

The conflict between Manaf and Ashwari was merely a blip in the news cycle of the Western world. Until soccer moms everywhere became invested in the story of a secret princess hiding in America and returning to her war-torn country.

The men talked about the potential lack of diplomacy and possible political unrest in Eastern Africa, while the entertainment cycles attempted to piece together the Queen's journey, as well as when and how the couple fell in love.

She had no fear of admitting to her illegal upbringing in America, especially since it was indirectly caused by her mother the Queen's denied request for asylum. Once America had the guarantee that the country of Manaf could secure it safely and relatively quickly, without the aid of American troops, the Queen's request was granted.

Overnight it seemed there was a change in perception of Ashwari by the nations that surrounded it, and by the ones that surrounded Manaf. Suddenly this tiny nation had a more powerful ally than the country that had conquered it.

She returned to Ashwari one week later, her entire family in tow. Her surrogate mother and father couldn't miss the opportunity to see Ashwari's first ceremony as a Manafi commonwealth.

"I was raised by Ashwari parents in America," Queen Asha began, her first official address as Queen to the Ashwari people. Zara was there to translate into Swahili.

"We ate Ashwari food, told Ashwari stories. We listened to the elders talk about how they 'got out.' Other than that we didn't talk about the rebellion, only as a way to explain why we were in America, and no longer in the country that we all dearly loved, even though most of us had never set foot here."

Her surrogate parents looked on in wonder. Back home after 30 years away was surreal enough, but now it was as if her mother was seeing the Queen on her throne, her *dnake*, her sister.

Her father felt proud seeing Gabby's poised demeanor as she addressed her people. He felt relieved seeing her so at home in her role.

"I spent 2.5 years here," she continued, "I know it sounds unbelievable, but part of me remembers that time. Part of me remembers servants. And wandering great halls in the middle of the night. Being back here feels like a dream, but it also feels like a completion.

"Until the day I met my husband, I didn't know who I was. My foster parents never told me who I truly was. When the King of Manaf explained that he wanted an alliance between my country and his, I didn't hesitate. I didn't know him from Adam, but I knew that I had to do what I could to save my country." She eyed her handsome Manafi King as she spoke.

"And so I left my Ashwari community in America, to leave with this... very ugly man and marry him," she said. She paused and heard laughter as Zara began to translate. The audience began to whoop and she laughed, hearing the native sound of Ashwari gladness that she recognized from her own community. She relaxed even more.

"I did what I had to do to take my rightful place as the daughter of an Otieno. I believe that my mother and my father, wherever they are, have both conspired to urge me on in this my entire life. Even when I didn't know who they were. And that they are at peace now. And my mother's spirit can rest."

Gabby stopped, feeling overwhelmed at her own words and the warmth of the crowd as they whooped and whooped for what seemed like ages. She felt both larger and smaller than life in that moment.

She swallowed a big lump as she continued, braving her surrogate mother's face. It nearly ripped her heart out to empty out a lifetime's worth of gratitude, but her parents deserved to know, truly know, what they had managed to do.

"Leonida," she called her by name. "*Ema...* I know my mother is proud of what you did for her. You kept me safe. You raised me with my mother's Ethiopian heritage and Ashwari's tradition. You are strong, you are brave."

She turned to her father. "Isaias... *Baba*, they tell me that my real father was ruthless. Sometimes I fear that I carry his ruthless way inside me. His jealousy, his pride, and paranoia. When I faced General Olayinka for the second time, before he stood trial and was convicted by the people, he said he could see it too," she revealed. A hush fell over the crowd at her words.

"He may have only said it to wound me, but he knew the man well. And I didn't. And I'm glad that I didn't, because I don't think he would have been a good father to me. So it was lucky that you raised me. So that I could do this job, not only with the blood of an Otieno, but with the loyalty and compassion of an Ayenew. Thank you, *Baba*."

The crowd whooped again in her parents' honor, and this time, Queen Asha joined in.

Join the Mailing List!

If you like what you've read, I would like to keep in touch with you!

- Find out about new releases, limited time deals and bonus content!
- Get access to fan exclusives from this and previous releases!
- Get to know me and what I'm up to, and even work with me as part of my Advance Team!

Simply click on the link, and enter your email address to sign up:

https://www.subscribepage.com/CLDMLLanding

I Love Reviews!

Yes, even the critical ones (sort of)! Did you like the book? Which part was your favorite? Was the sex too much? Not enough? Anything stand out to you that you've never read before, or haven't seen in awhile? Anything you could've done without, perhaps? Well, I wanna know!!

Besides that, when it comes to choosing the next great read, reviews can make or break, whether you're an indie author like me, or one of the big fish in a New York Publisher's pond.

Believe it or not, you can help. A LOT.

And all it will cost you is about a dozen words or more.

If you enjoyed this book at all, and think others should too, please take five minutes to leave this book a review on the page of your respective ebook retailer. Thank you!

About the Author

You can connect with me on:

🌐 https://cldonley.com/home

🐦 https://twitter.com/C_L_Donley

📘 https://facebook.com/amarascalling

Subscribe to my newsletter:

✉ https://www.subscribepage.com/CLDMLLanding

Also by C. L. Donley

Check out my fan favorites!

Leftovers With Benefits

When Kenya's husband Cecil unexpectedly leaves her for a white woman, she finds solace with the most unlikely new ally: Kevin Hayes, the other woman's ex.

The Book of Adam and Jo

When former klansman and white supremacist Adam Kerr meets a black single mother named Jo Abrams, their chemistry is instant despite their differences. A steamy, emotional read!

The Billionaire's Club Trilogy

Amara and Grayson: the hot, quirky couple that started it all. Mya and Dale: the controversial pairing that no one saw coming, especially the two of them. Kim and Bel: the undercover royals who fall in love at first sight.

Spend all day in la la land jet setting with this "plane Jane meets billionaire" trilogy about three couples that are as different as the individuals are from each other. Exotic locales, destination weddings, sex contracts, secret babies, and all the "happily ever afters" you could ever want!